For Maria, as ever.

EX LIBRIS

Last Days
Days
in
Cleaver
Square

PATRICK McGRATH

HUTCHINSON
LONDON

1 3 5 7 9 10 8 6 4 2

Hutchinson
20 Vauxhall Bridge Road
London SW1V 2SA

Hutchinson is part of the Penguin Random House group
of companies whose addresses can be found at
global.penguinrandomhouse.com

First published in the United Kingdom by Hutchinson in 2021

www.penguin.co.uk

A CIP catalogue record for this book is available from
the British Library.

ISBN 9781786332745

Typeset in 12.5/16 pt Baskerville MT Std
by Integra Software Services Pvt. Ltd, Pondicherry

Printed and bound in Great Britain by Clays Ltd, Elcograf S.p.A.

The authorised representative in the EEA is Penguin Random House
Ireland, Morrison Chambers, 32 Nassau Street, Dublin D02 YH68.

Penguin Random House is committed to a sustainable future for
our business, our readers and our planet. This book is made from
Forest Stewardship Council® certified paper.

1

Hard now to forget the first time I found him in the house. In the *house!* Of course I told Gilly at once. It was after dinner and we were sitting outside on the terrace. We are often out on the terrace in the summer. There's weeds coming up between the flagstones but it's handy for the garden because I can still get down the steps to the yard, which is where I keep my pots and urns and bags of manure and such. A warm evening, the air groggy with floral odours, in particular the Spanish jasmine, to my nose most pungent of them all.

– Gillian, I said.

– Pa.

– Something rather peculiar has happened.

– Oh?

– This so-called apparition.

– Yes?

– I've seen him again.

I lifted my glass. My hand was steady. Rather discoloured, of course, all blues and purples – I am old! – and spotted with blemishes and moles now, but yes: steady. The other one, my so-called apparition, he has to clamp his hand to the table to keep it still, and when he offers the Fascist salute the lifted arm will apparently tremble like a leaf in a gale! My gaze was fixed on a soughing tree at the end of the garden. A faint cry issued from somewhere nearby, plaintive, full of yearning, probably only a bird. I set down my glass and turned to Gilly.

– Where this time? she said.

– End of my bed.

– Oh no, Pa!

She rose to her feet, for this was new, and it rattled her. Christ alive, it rattled me! But she was alarmed. It was exasperating for her but what was I to do? Who else could I talk to? The other times it had always been from a bus, or in the street, as he turned a corner, and when I reached the corner he was gone.

– Oh yes. He was in his uniform.

Small exhalation, in fact a groan. It was the uniform of a highly decorated military officer, I told her, a general, in fact, with a small moustache, and heavy-lidded eyes, and a nose curved like a little sickle. Yes, himself. The fabric was green serge and considerably stained with sweat, blood, soil, faeces, who knows what? The cap had a stiff peak and a foliated Spanish eagle in gold over six-pointed stars all tarnished and chipped. You see, I miss nothing. That is because I am a poet. Habit of a lifetime.

2

So. Fraying dark blue sash, badly rusted medals, red tassels, gold piping, various arm-of-service insignia and crossed muskets under a double bugle with a red diamond on each collar point. Riding boots, filthy, as though he'd come through a cowshed or a military toilet. He was decrepit and unclean, he was sickly looking, falling apart, in fact, and he stank.

– God, Pa, and he was in your *bedroom*?

Yes, and I'd sat up in bed greatly startled and brought the bedsheet to my nose.

– Did he say anything to you?

– Oh yes.

– What?

– I don't want to tell you now. I'll tell you later.

– Tell me now.

– He was weeping, I said.

Gilly gazed out into the garden with one hand rather melodramatically clamped on top of her head, as though to prevent her thoughts from escaping, they were in such ferment. Then she turned. I was sitting with my own hands clutched in my lap, and oh, practically *beseeching* sympathy; or understanding, at the least. She seized me by the shoulders.

– Weeping?

– For Luis Carrero Blanco.

– Pa, you have to see someone. This can't go on.

I dropped my eyes. I nodded. But inwardly I was seething. I saw him, he was there. We spoke, yes, in Spanish, and it was about Luis Carrero Blanco, dead now of course. Close to the *generalísimo* since the early

3

days in North Africa, he told me. Huge bomb went off right under his car, Christmas before last, just after he came out of Mass, and some rich irony here, I thought, I mean the very idea that that black soul might escape the fires of hell, *I doubt it!* The Basques did it, of course. *Los vascos.* How they hated the bastard. And why? I asked him. He said nothing. Will I tell you? I said. Will I remind you what you did in Bilbao in the summer of 1937? And Guernica before that? *Guernica?* Oh, he didn't like that. They had to be punished, he said. Annihilated.

– Annihilated? I said. *¿Aniquilados?* All of them?

– *¡Sí! ¡Sí!*

Gillian said later she'd have made light of the whole thing, had it come from anyone else. But it was me, her father, and the utter conviction with which I described this *apparition* – as she insisted on calling it – left her in no doubt as to at least the reality of my emotion, if not, oh God no, of the event itself.

– Who else knows?

– Other than you? Nobody. You think I don't know how this sounds?

– And Finty?

– Finty?

– Your sister. The marine painter—

– I know who Finty is, darling.

She'd wandered a little way along the terrace, pushing her hands through her hair now. She sank down by a pot of night-scented stock and inhaled. Dusk was coming on, and in the west the sky was catching fire in

4

the last of the sun and picking up the blonde streaks in Gilly's hair. She has lovely hair, and her skin is so fair as at times to seem almost translucent. I glared at her. My hands were gripped tight to the fraying arms of the old wicker chair, and I felt my nose starting to run. Slight allergy to something in the garden, probably *el galán de noche*, which I believe to be a form of Spanish jasmine.

– You are not to tell anyone, Gilly. Not Finty, not Percy, not anyone, do you hear?

– Why not? Wipe your nose, Pa.

She is a handsome woman, and she knows it, but oh, she can be so very brisk with me at times. Fortunately my skin is thicker than it looks.

– They will think I'm hysterical. That's not what you think, is it, Gilly?

I was on my feet by this time. I flung a cigarette between my teeth and lit it with shaky fingers. I too have good hair, silver, and I wear it rather long, always have. I am a tall man, with a high forehead, I have a long, finely chiselled nose and a firm chin. Rather thin, intelligent lips. A desiccated fellow, I suppose you might say, although there was a time the blood ran quick in my veins like a torrent. *El torrente*, that was me. I pushed my fingers through my hair now, being perturbed. Gillian chose her words with care. She spoke quietly.

– Papá, General Franco is not in London. He cannot travel. He is dying.

She thought I didn't know? The infections, the ulcers, the wanderings of his ageing, failing mind, she thought I hadn't seen it for myself? The unsteady gait, how careful he'd been as he came round the side of the bed, and seated himself beside me, laid a thin trembling hand on my knee—?

– Then how do you explain it?

Staring straight ahead now I raised the cigarette to my lips. Steady as the Rock of Gibraltar. All at once something moved in the deepening shadows in the garden. It was happening more often now, and I leaned forward so as to alert Gilly.

– *See?* I whispered.

– What?

– Shadows concealing movement.

Avatars of death, is what I really meant, but she wouldn't have understood. I hadn't expected them until winter.

– What?

I sat back.

– Nothing, dear.

So we settled into silence, Gillian still aghast at this apparently shocking revelation and quietly rubbing her fingers together, as her quick suspicious mind ran through the options, I could see it happening. Finally she told me I must have imagined the whole thing. Wasn't that what I would have said, in her place?

– I'm not in your place, dear, I said. I'm in my own place, and I saw him. I want to go in now.

– You don't think it was an apparition then?

– Am I an apparition to you?

– He's in Madrid. People have seen him.

– That was the apparition.

I regretted this at once. It was wild talk.

– Oh for Christ's sake! So what do you think he wants then?

I rose from my chair. A long, bony finger, my own, quivered beneath my daughter's chin.

– *Exactly!*

2

I FLUNG ASIDE the newspaper. It was high summer but in London great winds were blowing. Governments were collapsing. Change was in the air. The Germans no longer felt guilty about the war. I paced around the house. I was vexed, unsettled; preoccupied. It was only four in the afternoon. Some obscure piece of modern music was playing on the radio. I turned it off. I paused in the kitchen to gaze out at our old trees, dense with foliage and all flapping about at the end of my busy garden. There goes the squirrel! Here come the pigeons! The temperature rose and the sky grew darker still. A thunderstorm seemed to threaten but never arrived. I heard a key scraping in the unyielding front door, then a strangled blasphemy—

– Gilly, darling? I shouted. Is that you?

I hauled the front door open. Gillian entered and wrestled from her shoulder a basket full of books which she then dumped in a heap on the floor, including a short history of the Spanish Civil War, although why she needed a book on the subject when she has me in the house, who was there—? She stood in front of the mirror, panting. She'd been in the London Library, she said. Her hair had come seriously adrift in the wind.

– Look at the state of me, she said.

– Oh, just come in and have a drink, dear. I can see we've both had a bloody day.

Daughter turned to father, laid a hand on my cheek.

– You had a bloody day, Pa?

– Nightmare of a day, I said.

We went through to the sitting room.

– Any news? I said, once we were settled with drinks.

She wandered over to the window. The trees were still whipping about, for the wind was boisterous as ever.

– I think I might marry Percy Gauss, she said.

– Sir Percy, I said faintly. Could do worse, I suppose.

I will not deny the sensation: a chill finger to the heart. It was nearly seven years since she'd been abandoned by William Culvert from the Treasury Office and moved in with her old pa. I'd been living alone for some years, except for Dolores López, of course, who's down in the basement, my housekeeper. Without my help Dolores would never have got out of Madrid, after her family were all killed. She was only eight years old then. Been with me ever since, almost forty years now. But my manner of existence had become irksome to me, or rather, living alone with only Dolores López for company had become irksome to me, for I'd never been what you'd call a domesticated sort of a man, nor a solitary man, nor even a particularly cordial or convivial or *nice* sort of a man. I was still writing, it's true, and thank the Christ for it, but the current book, as I'd told Gilly – a slim volume of my late, uncollected verse – would be my last. She said she'd heard that before.

So she moved in with me, into this faded Georgian pile in this unkempt old square off the Kennington Road, not so far from Vauxhall Bridge. Been in the family for years, since my father's day, and falling apart, rather, but it does at least have a nice walled garden at the back, my own private arcadia, I think it – last living jungle in south London, ha. A small untidy lawn and a profusion of bushes and trees, viper's bugloss, lilac, phlox, plumbago, agapanthus, and so on. Jasmine, silver birches – a high sprawl of pink-and-white hydrangeas with concealed among them a little stagnant pond all dankness and mystery. Nice seedy pub across the square, the Earl of Rochester, and we're not far from the Imperial War Museum, once a great asylum, of course, where Gilly can catch the bus to work and be at the Foreign Office in fifteen minutes. There is also a cemetery. Noreen McNulty, Gillian's late mother, sleeps there. Sometimes walks there. I wanted to talk more about Percy Gauss but Gilly evidently didn't. Rather abruptly she changed the subject.

– You know about the courts martial, she said, settling in an armchair and flattening her skirt on her knees.

Yes I did. All too grimly familiar. Men had been sentenced to death, more to follow. Basques, in the main, and one young anarchist, from Barcelona, Salvador Puig Antich. Him I cannot bear to think about yet.

– Of course. But, Gilly, tell me—

– Oh, they'll never let him die. That bloody man.

That bloody man, yes. This was a conversation we'd had before. I was coming to believe that a diabolical bargain had been struck, the tribute to be paid being the raddled soul of old pagan Spain, and in exchange, eternal life for this monster, this tinpot dictator who clings to power like a *limpet*, his sole intention to keep alive the shoddy trappings of an exhausted fascism responsible for atrocities unnumbered over forty years. Yes, forty long years. And why should I remember what he's done, or care, even? Nobody else does. It is all peace and reconciliation now, all best forgotten. Ha. Not by me.

But death be not proud, I thought. Take him now before he can do any more damage. Or to be precise, before he can do old Francis McNulty any more damage, for I am frankly haunted.

3

I HAD RECOGNISED him at once. This is the first time I'm talking about now, a few days after I'd come upon a scrap of serge in the garden, torn from his uniform by a dog perhaps, or on a piece of barbed wire. I was on the top deck of a bus coming over Lambeth Bridge, and he was shuffling off down Horseferry Road towards the police courts. He had his back to me, but I couldn't mistake him even in a gabardine raincoat and a bowler hat, that corpulent little monstrosity. He was the epitome of banality and you saw it in his gait, he had the mincing step of a pouter pigeon but oh, with a murderous heart of hardest stone within. My bus was making the wide turn onto the Embankment but I was already halfway down the stairs, shouting at the conductor to let me off, I'd missed my stop! It was the middle of August, and raining.

But when I got off the bus he was nowhere to be seen.

There's a bank just down from the corner and I went in. Long queues for the tellers' windows but no little Spaniard in a bowler hat. Several heads turned as I stood gasping and staring about me, rather unkempt and dishevelled, I dare say, an old fellow in some serious disarray! Then back out again onto the street, and still no sign of him. But there is of course a church just there, St Francis Xavier, so in I went to get out of the rain.

A funeral was in progress. It was ill-attended, say the least. There was a coffin on a pair of trestles in front of the altar. A thin Jesuit in black vestments stood facing the congregation, which numbered exactly seven, counting myself. The wheezing organ in the choir overhead ceased wheezing as I entered, and by long habit I dipped my fingers in the holy water, then wiped them on my trousers. I did not attempt a genuflection, not with these knees. I sat in the back pew. Two mourners stood at the front, the widow, I presumed, in a black veil, with a young woman beside her. An older man in a grey suit stood three pews behind them, and, oddly, he bore a resemblance to my father, and I shivered. Uncanny. Why would he be here?

On the other side of the aisle, a few pews further back, stood a pair of middle-aged men in wet raincoats, and behind them was a woman of about sixty in a coat with a damp fur collar and a black hat with a feather in it that had once been gay. She too was familiar to me, but I couldn't think where I'd seen her before. My second wife, Noreen, Gilly's mother, had worn a hat like that. All a bit unsettling, and I am not a man easily rattled.

There was a low murmur of the Latin canon now. It was a simple coffin with one limp bunch of flowers laid upon it, and what kind of a life were we mourning here, I thought, that this sad piece of theatre was the extent of his obsequies? Seven of us in a gloomy damp Catholic church half a mile from Westminster Abbey, where some years previously Winston Churchill – no friend to men like me, ha! – had set off in a flag-draped coffin, and a million mourners lined the route. Hard not to remember Ozymandias:

> *I met a traveller from an antique land,*
> *Who said: Two vast and trunkless legs of stone,*
> *Stand in the desert—*

And on it goes, until Shelley's lovely great shout of doom:

> *My name is Ozymandias, king of kings:*
> *Look on my works, ye Mighty, and despair!*

Bracing stuff. I came late to the Romantics myself. But in that gloomy church near Lambeth Bridge, that damp Thursday in the summer of 1975, I saw no sign of Ozymandias, nor of the *generalísimo*, but somehow I could not seem to rise from my pew and leave the place. The priest had embarked on his homily, a passage from St John the Divine with which I was once familiar. He did not have a ringing voice, say the least, and it was dubious that he had known the deceased man well, if at all. But presumably one of the mourners in attendance had given him a few memories with which to fashion a tribute. I then found myself bowed over in my pew with my head in my hands, and for the usual reason, tears.

Later I told Gilly about it and she was on to me at once.

– Did you cry, Pa?

I admitted I had but for once she didn't laugh at me, no scorn at all, in fact. I told her I'd lit a few candles for the soul of the departed, and she asked me if I'd waited to see the coffin carried out and I told her I hadn't. There didn't seem enough bearers on hand to carry the poor man anywhere, I said. But I think she understood that her old pa could not attend even a stranger's funeral without perforce contemplating his own end. Nor did she ask me why I'd entered St Francis Xavier in the first place, which was tactful of her. I was raised in the Roman faith, so was she, but I had long since rejected the teachings of that church, of all churches, in fact. All heap bad opium to my mind, proud godless heathen I am.

But that poor man with his seven mourners – a widow, deserted, I imagined. A grown daughter, no doubt in full possession of the facts of her parents' wretched marriage. A brother, himself perhaps alienated from the widow and her daughter, this all seemed clear enough. Two men in raincoats from the pub where he drank. And the other woman, with the hat? She was the other woman. Stood by him as best she could. Loved him in her way. You could do worse. And I the seventh. There was a poem here, nice little lament, or an elegy, something in the

15

manner of Gerard Hopkins, perhaps. *Oh he is dead then, Herbert Hake, the fishmonger?*

I'd left shortly after, stepped out onto the Horseferry Road, where it was still raining, thinking, what am I doing? Elderly party leaps off bus to pursue what, a hallucination? – a *delusion?* – through the wet streets of Westminster, so as to then what? – denounce to the civil authorities a little chap in a bowler hat for *war crimes?* I went out into the falling rain and hurried homeward over Lambeth Bridge, beneath which the Thames was surging, roiling in strong winds like a great thick soup coming to the boil. Then overhead, suddenly, a roll of booming thunder, and a vivid flash that slashed the sky for one brief moment, like a spout of cosmic glory, as of some vast whale breaching in the firmament—!

4

LATE THAT SAME night had come the knock on the
door. Gilly had gone up an hour before. I was still
in my study. I went out into the hall. I was not expecting anybody, not at that time of the night. Faint sense
of dread, I will admit, in light of the day's funereal
events. I flung open the front door. The rain had eased
off and was now dripping steadily into the gutters and
down the drains and onto the steps, where stood a figure
holding a stick and shrouded in deep shadow in a long
black raincoat, slick and wet, collar turned up, hat pulled
low. Nearby stood a large black suitcase. My heart sank.
Death had come calling. My turn, I thought, now I'm
for it, off to no-man's-land in a big black suitcase. The
figure turned towards me—

Oh bathos. My sister.

– Hello, Francis.

– Christ, Finty, you gave me a shock—!

With an ugly belching sound the drainpipe disgorged onto the doorstep a watery pudding of dead leaves.

– I might have known, I said. This is Gillian's doing?

– Francis, I'm soaked. Can I please come in?

I stepped aside to let my sister enter her childhood home, and with no good grace, I can tell you, for she had alarmed me, coming so late and with no warning. I have had three sisters in my time, only one still living, Finty, the one who left London to go to the Isle of Mull to paint the sea. Every December she comes south by way of Edinburgh, where she boards an overnight express after some hours in the company of her old artist pals, those who are with us still. But it wasn't December. It was late August.

She hung her wet things in the hall then shuffled through to the kitchen. She's been walking with a stick for some years now. Arthritic knees, poor old girl, hips a bit dodgy too. I put the kettle on. I got the milk out. You ask me how I've kept my anger alive as long as I have? When so many seem to want just to forget? It is buried very deep, so deep in fact that powerful engines of excavation are required to create any disturbance in me these days. For the most part I am the capable, dutiful, unjustly neglected old poet who sits and listens to people with grievances, or points to make, or who have time to waste, or whatever the bloody hell it was that brought my sister to my door in the middle of the night.

– Dear old Fint, I said, I don't know what your plans are, but I'm going to bed.

18

She was exhausted. In her eighties now, but her mind still clear as a glass of gin unlike some I could name.

– Off you go then, she said. I'll be up later.

– Francis, are you awake?

My reverie is fled. Someone is tapping at my chamber door.

– Come in then.

The door cracks open. What can she want now? It's after midnight and I'm in bed with James Hogg.

– Are you alone?

What a wag. Gilly has the biggest bedroom in the house but mine I think is the better one. It used to be my father's after Mummy left us. The curtains are of heavy maroon velvet, threadbare rather in places, and with some moth damage. They are pulled closed and a small coal fire burns in the grate near the bed for I am always cold now, even in summer. Close to the fireplace is an old wing chair upholstered in some kind of gold-threaded material, fraying at the edges, and often occupied by my cat, the ageing Henry Threshold, a cantankerous animal. And beside the wing chair a small lamp on a table. Also on the table there's an engraved silver tray presented to me in 1954 by the London Ambulance Service. Also, a decanter of sherry.

– Come in, for God's sake, shut the door, there's a draught. Do you want a glass of sherry?

No she does not.

– So you're reading the great man, she says, when she's settled herself in the wing chair, and with no small effort, for her legs were stiff and painful after the walk from the Tube. Now who is it you remind me of? Tell me, Francis, do you think you're losing your mind?

Dear God but I despair of these women who abandon their filters in age and just say whatever comes into their heads.

Later, when she's gone, I put the guard on the fire and turn off the lamp. But I cannot sleep. Have I spoken of the slow fuse that smoulders so deep inside me that it takes a month to rouse so much as a spark? Other times, but they are rare, I make up my mind on the instant, and not without a charge of irritation attached. This had been one of them.

– No, dear, I'd said, with some crispness of tone, I am remarkably astute still. Is that why you're here?

– Is that so?

– I miss nothing. Why do you ask?

She'd taken a pencil from her pocket and was fingering it as though it were a cigarette. Absently she made a business of smelling it. She was of course forbidden to smoke upstairs.

– I heard something.

A shrug here, as though it were nothing. Gossip below stairs. I don't trust her an inch. She's heard about me seeing the *generalísimo* on Lambeth Bridge, or God forbid, coming to my bedroom at night. Who told her? Who's the spy? Gilly, obviously. Dolores López knows but she won't breathe a word. I watch my sister closely. She's a tall, skinny old girl in a tweed jacket and brown corduroy trousers, long restless hands stained yellow, rings on every finger. Hair tied up in a bandanna and clear, fierce blue eyes like mine. You'd know us anywhere as brother and sister, lanky, beaky customers with these piercing eyes and silver hair. Encrustations at the corners of her mouth, food, blood. Paint. She speaks in quick cultivated tones, as do I, I suppose, and despite everything we still like each other, well, she looked after me when I was a boy, after Mummy ran off with Roger Dixon. But I won't confide in her about my *apparition*, so called.

– What did you hear?

– Oh, it's cagey we're being, is it? she said. Well. I won't harass you, dear man. My God, I forget what a nice big bed this is. I say, move over.

I moved over and she clambered up onto the bed, on her knees and elbows, much cursing and gasping, spilling only a drop or two of the small glass of amontillado she'd decided she wanted after all. She took my hand. Together we gazed at the ceiling. It has a decorated moulding which in direct sunlight creates a horizontal shadow, and at night, with the fire burning, there's a lovely sombre flickering effect. I knew she liked the room, in fact she liked the whole house, and she was right to, it is a peaceful house, or it was until recently, but yes, a fine old Georgian pile with long windows and high chimneys, it's the house we grew up in. Finty was here when Dolores first arrived, after I saved her life in Spain in the war. All London brick and the facade plastered although flaking a bit and showing its age, well, who isn't? She once told me she never minded leaving London so much as she minded leaving this

21

house, although by then she'd found the Isle of Mull and liked it better.

Now she was lying beside me in bed in the firelight and enquiring as to my sanity. I told her about a reporter who'd showed up a few days before to ask me about Spain. The awakening Spain, apparently. Awakening? You call it sleep, then, what came before, I'd said, children starving in the streets, rooting about in slop pails for a scrap of peel or a snail? Their mothers whoring, the prisons overflowing, summary executions – don't get me started on Spain!

– Brave of him to try that with you, she said.

– I wouldn't talk to him.

She levered herself up off the pillow and brushed a wisp of hair from my cheek.

– You saw him off yourself, did you, Francis?

– I don't think you find that very hard to believe.

This made her snort. Then out she rolled from under the blanket and drank her sherry sitting on the edge of the bed with her back to me. She set the glass down on the bedside table, saying she'd forgotten to tell me what I reminded her of, as I lay adrift in big pillows reading Hogg, but she'd remember in the morning. Then she leaned over me again and kissed my forehead, as she had when I was a child. She said she'd ask Dolores if I'd lost my mind, it was no use talking to me.

5

Yes I'd seen him off myself. In fact there were two of them. I'd seen them both off. There'd been fresh speculation in the press about the *generalísimo*'s failing health and a reporter from the *Manchester Guardian* had come to the house. And why? The poetry, of course. You think about the Spanish Civil War, the poetry that came out of it? You think of me. He'd brought a photographer. I wasn't expecting them. I'd forgotten they were coming. I was at the front door shouting at them and Gilly could hear me from upstairs. I was being quite reasonable, so I thought, considering the young man had asked me if I planned to go back to Spain.

– I've told you, I said, as I stood there on my doorstep – it was a Saturday, around eleven in the morning, and raining – I've told you already, I said, that there's no memory I possess that isn't tainted regarding Spain, but do you listen to me? No you do not. Why not go back?

you say. *He's dying.* But I heard them in the streets of Madrid, I say, and you know what they were shouting? *Viva la Muerte.* That's right. Long live Death. *Falangistas*, of course, Franco's thugs. Necrophiliac inanity, as old Miguel called it. Would you please stop that?

I was speaking to the photographer, who was snapping away as though I'd told him he could and I hadn't. It was raining quite hard now and I knew they wanted to come in but I'd decided against it.

– He may be dying, I said, but he won't *go*! I still see him! Where is Gilly? I thought you wanted to just let sleeping dogs lie? Lie, lie, lie—

I turned away, lifting my hands, shaking my head as though to say, am I to have no peace at all? But the whole performance crumbled when Gilly came downstairs and quietly told me that they were expected, and that I should let them in. She mentioned later that there were at least two cigarettes on the go, one in my hand and one in the ashtray on the table under the mirror by the front door, where the pair from the *Manchester Guardian* stood like deer in bright headlights, and I don't even smoke! I suppose I should have had them in but I didn't want to.

– I should like to tell you something, I said.

By this time Gilly had got them in from the rain and we were in the sitting room.

– I knew a man who went to Spain with an ambulance unit, and the Fascists put him up against a wall, you see, and they would have shot him. But something happened and they didn't.

24

– What happened, sir?

I gave him one of my fierce looks. I'd rather taken to him, the young reporter, now that they were in the house. Gilly was at the drinks table making a bit of a clatter so I knew that serious hospitality was in the offing. It was almost lunchtime.

– He came back to London – what's wrong with that story? I'm an old man.

The boy reporter was scribbling away in his little notebook and the photographer was taking snaps again.

– Go on, please, said the boy, whose name was Hugh Supple. He certainly looked supple to me. Were you tortured? he said. You once said you were tortured.

I leaned over and gripped his knee.

– I could say, Hugh, I said quietly, that this man I'm talking about went to Spain with an ambulance unit to help the people of Madrid, and he was taken prisoner and unspeakable things were done to him. All right?

– But what—

– What unspeakable things? If I told you, they wouldn't be unspeakable, well, would they? I'd have spoken them. I'd have made them *speakable* and the point is that they're not.

I was peering into his face. He had skin like milk and thick wild hair the colour of good soil. How old was he – twelve? Did he even shave? Then I released his knee and sat back. All the killing in Spain was done by boys like this.

– Is it because he's dying? Franco, I mean?

– He was always dying. In the *heart*, you understand?

I laid a hand on my own heart by way of illustration.

– Thank you, dear. Not too much tonic now.

This last was addressed to Gilly, who'd appeared at my elbow with a glass. Gin would sometimes calm me down at lunchtime. More trouble than it was worth to try and argue with me, she said later, and this boy wasn't up to it. He wasn't even trying. What worried Gilly, she told me when they'd gone, was that these angry outbursts were becoming more frequent, and it was hard on Dolores López. You can't expect people just to put up with it, not as I do, said Gilly, well, I'm your daughter. I don't actually have a lot of choice.

I was astonished. Angry? I hadn't been angry!

– Now come on, darling, I said, it wasn't that bad, was it?

– Yes, Papá, it was, those poor men standing out in the rain and you ranting at them, it wasn't their fault. One of these days you'll go out through the front door and small boys will throw stones at you.

– Oh what, I said, and shout, Witch, Witch?

And who'll protect me from that, I thought, you? Oh no, you'll be off somewhere with *Percy Gauss*, ha.

– And it's not as if I don't have a life of my own, you said, as though to confirm my worst fears.

There was another silence. Hovering unspoken was the information you'd given me a few days earlier, and which we hadn't yet discussed. You were going to marry Percy Gauss. I could weep. The radio was scraping away, that damn violin sonata again. Gilly yawned.

– You used to like talking to the press, she said.

26

– That was when I had something to say to the press. Those days are over.

– So you say. Are you ready for lunch?

Prokofiev. How I used to love him. Now he gives me the creeps.

Later I went upstairs for my siesta but I didn't sleep. Young Hugh Supple had awoken memories. I'd once told Gilly I would never have believed that someone who'd suffered as I had could feel guilt as a result. But it was the case. Why should that be so? It compounds the insult. Why couldn't I just let it go, like everybody else? Nobody in Spain talks about the civil war, they tell me – keep your mouth shut, pretend it didn't happen. All too complicated, everybody guarded and silent and afraid, especially those who were on the winning side who have good reason to fear reprisal. I read the Spanish papers.

So yes, let it go, old man. Just bury it – all that *guilt* – deep as possible, preferably in an unmarked grave. Well, I thought I had. But some fool child comes knocking at the door and it was lucky Gilly was at home or who knows what might have happened. The problem with the press is, I can't control the conversation any more.

Now I couldn't sleep because I felt it stirring in the depths. I glimpsed an old farm building on Suicide Hill with its roof blown off and shell-holes in the walls and the floor thick with plaster and lumps of concrete and dying men. Cold rain beating down. I could smell shit. Everything smells of shit in a war. And blood. And iodine and smoke and death – the furtive odour, so called. The man I'm thinking about was lying slumped on the floor with blood in his mouth and God knows what else – the Moors had used him for a latrine although I haven't ever told Gilly that. I haven't told a living soul. Don't imagine I ever will.

6

G ILLY WAS PLEASANTLY surprised when I told her that her Auntie Finty had appeared in the middle of the night and was asleep in the attic. I mentioned it to her before she left for work.

– Oh, she must be exhausted, poor thing, she said.

Never an early riser, my sister, put it mildly. She wouldn't be down for hours yet.

– You must have put the wind up her, I said.

– Oh, Papá.

– Yes, oh, Papá. What did you say, Gillian? Did you tell her I was demented?

Gilly never looks her best in the morning. It may be because she's very much the civil servant at this hour of the day. Pale, slim, long legs like all the McNulty women, but when she's in one of her stern grey skirts and flat heels, and a tailored black jacket over a starched white blouse, there's a birdlike quality. Her sharp little

29

eyes spark like a sparrow's and her nose is beaky, and that slight overbite suggests a rather *pecky* personality. I certainly thought it *pecky* of her to write to my sister and tell her I was senile.

– I said I was concerned about you, she said. I didn't suggest she drop everything and come to London.

– A great loss to British art, I said, old Finty McNulty absent from her easel for a week or two.

– Oh, Pa—

– I hope it's no more than that, I said. The nation would never forgive me.

– Pa, don't be so beastly. You're not altogether yourself these days – I only mentioned it in passing.

– If not myself, pray, who then am I?

– You forget things, and you make things up.

– What can you mean? What do I forget? What do I make up? I forget nothing!

But she was out in the hall by this time and peering into the mirror by the door. Her hair was scraped up tight and pinned at the back like some pricey punishment madam in Shepherd Market, and we know what they cost.

– I have to go.

The front door banged behind her.

Later I went out into the garden. After the rain the night before I wanted to have a look at my roses but I got distracted, oh, by the hydrangeas – for some reason they were not doing well – and I couldn't understand why so many things were dying – the ivy on the wall was *brown*! I pottered about with trug and trowel, sitting on a little wooden crate, and forgot about everything for an hour or so. And it was when I was bent over, up to the elbows in soil, that I glanced up and saw him again. Yes. Just standing there, in his uniform, as though lost in thought, with hydrangeas up to his waist. Not a leaf stirring, nor a blade of grass, and everything much darker than it should have been. I straightened my back, and on my crate still I sat gazing at him and remembered how he'd wept for Luis Carrero Blanco, and how it had affected me. It affected me now, for he looked, oh, so very *pitiful*, that ghastly little apparition, or whatever he was, standing in my flower bed. Later I sat on a damp bench and gazed at the place where I'd seen him, and although he'd been there only a moment, and in an evanescent sort of a way—

> *Before he drifted off*
> *So very desolate and lost*
> *I could almost see him there*
> *Still.*

I turned towards the house. A figure in black stood in the open French windows in the sitting room, gazing at me. It was Dolores López. All at once I knew without a shadow of a doubt that she too had seen him. I gazed at her, searching, I suppose, for a sign, but oh, inscrutable woman, in all the years she'd been living in my house only rarely had I caught so much as a glimpse of her private mind. But nor had I wanted to, until this moment, when it mattered to me what she'd seen. But even as I lifted my hand she turned away and went back into the house. Such an odd, occluded woman she was. I saved her life, did I mention this? Doc Roscoe and I, we got her out of a burning building during the bombing in Madrid. She was just a child then. I remember—

When Finty came downstairs she found me at the kitchen table, remembering. I rose to my feet and turned to the sink, for I confess I had been weeping a little. She offered to make me lunch. I told her I always had a sandwich for lunch now. I was frankly glad to see her for I had, yes, been rather shaken by what happened earlier. You ask me, my sister makes better sandwiches than she does paintings but what do I know? She opened the fridge and got out the cheese, the chutney, the butter, etc.

— You all right, dear? You look a bit peaky.
— I'm fine, I said. You sleep well?
— Like the dead.
Ha.

7

THE ROOM UPSTAIRS, the dining room, with the long table, which can seat eight, has hanging on its walls a number of seascapes and portraits, all painted by my sister and all second-rate, in my considered opinion – for which, as I say, I make no claims. Her room is at the very top of the house, in the attic, where she slept when we were children. There's a narrow staircase from the upstairs landing where crowded on the walls, on either side, on thin wire, hang her early drawings and watercolours and prints and such, all framed behind glass, most of them from before she found her so-called spiritual home on the Isle of Mull. I suppose one has to be respectful of the sort of drivel one's elder sibling spouts so I tend to keep quiet, and we've avoided the topic for the last fifty years. We rub along well enough, Finty and I, God knows we've looked out for each other long enough, in sickness and in health and so on. And

I do believe she would never let me down. But I didn't like this sudden unexpected appearance in the middle of the night, and I asked her, once we had our sandwiches in front of us, what she was here for.

She put down her glass and gazed at me. She was wearing a headscarf, a ropy cardigan and a tweed skirt. She looked rather *county*; distant cousin of the Queen, perhaps – not that I'm any friend of the monarchy, I'm the man who spits in his hanky whenever I go past the Palace. There was a glass of red wine in front of her, good stuff Gilly gets from a posh shop in Chelsea. She lifted it to her lips and, still staring at me, sipped. A silence ensued. She flattened her mouth and frowned. All at once I saw in my mind's eye a face, and it was a young Scots lad I used to know.

> *And when I think of all I've lost*
> *And all I've been forgiven*
> *I see my life as broken glass*
> *In the something Glens of Gideon*
> *And – da da, da da, etc.*

Where did *that* come from?! My own pen. I had a Hebridean romance of my own about a century ago. 'To the Glens of Gideon', I called it. I used to be able to write like that. Can't now. Age withers one in so many ways.

– What did Gilly say?

– That you were seeing things.

– You're a fine one to talk.

Oh, I'd irritated her, or hurt her feelings. I thought I'd press on anyway.

– But why, Finty, why on earth would a woman like yourself give the best years of her life to painting stormy seas on the Isle of bloody Mull, of all places?

I'd never put it so bluntly before.

– *Are* you seeing things, Francis?

Once I saw things nobody should ever have to see.

– Honestly, do you mean?

– Yes, dear, honestly, what do you think I mean?

She had tipped her head to one side and rested her thin, leathery old face on her bony old fingers, which were clasped under her chin, all beringed, her elbows on the table either side of her untouched sandwich, and was gazing at me with a kind of benign scepticism. I set my own elbows on the table and mirrored this sister of mine as best I could, in posture and expression. It was the doppelgänger game. We used to play it when we were children. At that moment Dolores López entered the kitchen through the door from the basement. She was astonished to see Finty rise from the table, and her face grew tender as she lifted her arms. The women embraced. They had of course been like mother and daughter, ever since Dolores came to Cleaver Square as a little girl. Now they held each other at arm's length, and with great warmth.

– ¿*Te quedarás?*

You'll stay?

– *Sí.*

Dolores closed her eyes for a second.

35

– *Después, Dolores, por favor*, I murmured, without taking my eyes from my sister's face.

– *Sí, señor.*

Clump clump clump.

– Oh, get on with it, you fool, said Finty, very slightly tearful, I thought.

– I have a night visitor sometimes, I said.

I lowered my head and clasped my skull with both hands, and thin strands of silver hair spilled through my fingers. I stared at her from lowered eyes, sheepish.

– What, here in the house?

– And in the street. Once or twice. And the garden.

– Who is he?

– I won't tell you.

– But he's not real.

I may have mentioned how slow I am to anger, but some unpleasant emotion was gathering inside me like a squall at sea and I wasn't sure I could contain it. Of course he was bloody real. I saw him!

– Francis McNulty, don't you *dare* lose your temper with me.

I stood up. I'd been drinking water but now I fetched out a wine glass and poured myself a good measure. I stood at the sink and stared out into the garden. If I were a smoker of cigarettes I would certainly have had one then.

– I don't know what he is.

I turned. Finty was troubled, then her face became full, oh, practically *overflowing* with affection and concern, damn it, because she was my sister and she loved me

36

like a firstborn son, she always had. Then she was sitting close beside me and asking me if I wanted her to help, what could she do? I told her I could manage. I was all right. And at that moment I was, I could.

– Honestly?

I was nodding away at her.

– Still, I might stay here for a bit.

– Oh, dear old Flint, please do stay for a bit.

There was another hug. Dear Flinty Fint. She was my sister, yes, but for much of my life she'd been a mother to me too.

8

WE CROSSED INTO Spain in the early winter of 1936, after several unsuccessful attempts, one of them involving a fishing boat in rough seas that was almost sunk by an Italian warship—

No, too soon! I throw down my pen. Not ready! Never be ready! I make sense of what I can but it's like trying to mend a broken window with fragments of glass that belong elsewhere, *and will not cohere.* Exhaustion, dust, filth, in convoy through the Guadarramas in a rattling old motor ambulance with a shot suspension, and the Moors already at the gates of Madrid and German bombers every night—

I am in bed now. I have taken my pill and turned off the lamp. Thinking *too soon*, I fall asleep. An hour later I am awoken by more loud shouting – and now it is myself who is shouting! – and I struggle, panicking, out of bed, and such a sight I make, I'm sure, as I descend the stairs, pyjamas flapping about me, and Gilly comes bleary-eyed out of her bedroom but not before I've got down the stairs and then I'm out through the front door into the wet night, and I'd have run all the way down Kennington Lane to Vauxhall Bridge and thrown myself in the river, yes I would, and drowned!

Instead I stand under a street lamp, barefoot, bent over in my pyjamas in the drizzling rain with my hands on my thighs, all cramped up and wheezing. I am aware of Gilly now with an umbrella and she's got her arm round me, so I lay my head on her shoulder and she helps me back into the house, where I collapse in a chair and sit with my head in my hands, weeping. Dolores López is in the hall and she wraps a blanket round me, and Finty has come downstairs and tries to comfort me, and I clutch her hands, such an old shipwreck I am, such a pitiful bloody display—

– Oh sweet Jesus, I whisper, that was bad.
– Was it him again?
– No!

They know I'm having a nightmare. I'm famous for them. I sit shivering uncontrollably, the cold so deep in my bones I feel I will surely die of it. Gilly gets some socks on my feet, and Dolores López comes back with a small glass of brandy. She's turned a lamp on, and a bizarre scenario comes to life, the three of them in dressing gowns throwing large shadows on the wall as they huddle around this gaunt old lunatic in a state of the most wretched distress—

– *Gracias, Dolores*, I whisper, still clutching her hands, and the glass, and bringing them together to my lips. Dear Dolores, I know she knows what I know. She knows he's here.

– Oh that's better, I murmur. Jesus Christ Almighty, that was a bad one.

Then it all comes back to me, and had Dolores not taken it from me the glass would surely have slipped from my fingers and shattered on the floor.

– You are awake now, she whispers, *está despierto, Señor Francisco, fue solamente una pesadilla*.

All just a bad dream.

– Yes yes, thank you, darling. Oh God, Gilly, I think I will have to sleep with you tonight.

– Yes, Papá, of course. Have you had a pill?

– I shall need another one.

– Dolores, dear, can you get Papá's white pills from his bathroom? And run the bath, please.

Dolores padded off upstairs. I put a hand to my forehead. Gilly sat gazing at me.

– I've woken the whole bloody house, I said.

We waited in silence for Dolores López to return. Then they helped me to my feet. I shook them off and tottered upstairs unaided, and across the landing to Gilly's bedroom. I paused in the doorway. At the foot of the stairs I saw Gilly exchange a glance with Finty, then both women lifted their eyes to heaven. I entered Gilly's bedroom and soon the house was quiet once more.

9

IT WAS THE Sunday morning. Gilly was at the kitchen table with the newspapers. I sat down and poured myself a cup of tea.

– I'm so sorry, darling, I said. Unforgivable.

I was my old self again, more or less. Less.

– What happened? You want to tell me?

– Too tedious.

She was silent. It was a damp, warm day. I wished to God the weather would change. I longed for winter. Perhaps then I could die. I certainly bloody hoped so. And winter's the time for it. There was mist drifting in the garden, making it seem unreal, somehow, the silver birch like a ghost with the mist clinging to it, hanging in shrouds in the pale thin branches.

– Where were you? she said at last.

– Some room in an old monastery where everything echoed. One of their night tribunals. Three men in uniform at a table, *falangistas*. Dead black eyes, nasty men. And the one in charge—

– The *generalísimo*?

– No. The *capitán*.

The young Spanish captain who was later taken prisoner and exchanged for one of ours. Doc Roscoe had to cut his leg off. I was there. But he was never in the monastery, apart from in my nightmare. I was alone in front of them – the others had all been taken away. I knew what was going to happen. I could hear the Angelus bell.

My tone was weary.

– I wanted to explain but I couldn't speak a word of Spanish, it was all gone, not a word. Then I realised, I don't know how, the way you do in dreams, that they weren't going to shoot me after all.

A pause here.

– It was the *garrote*.

I almost lost my composure. I touched my throat.

– Imagine!

Gilly found it hard to, but she knew about the *garrote* all right, thin wire round the throat, a stick in the wire at the back so the *verdugo* could twist it tight. Or an iron collar with a screw at the back, and he tightened it till your neckbone snapped—

But Gilly has never been much impressed by my dreams, lacks the imagination. Doesn't read my poetry either, probably because I'm not producing any. Never even read the sonnets. I won prizes for those sonnets—!

– There was a *verdugo* in the courtroom, that's how I knew, I said. That's what woke me up.

– ¿*Verdugo*?

– Executioner. With a wire. Thin man, bad teeth, some of them black, some missing. Wrapping the wire round his fist then unwrapping it and starting all over again.

– Papá, it was only a dream.

I cast upon my daughter rather a cold eye. I felt she was trying to rob me of something, not some precious treasure, nothing like that, but a very real kind of terror which I had known as a young man in Spain. Only a dream, ha. History just a dream, I suppose, tell that to Doc Roscoe, tell him it was all a dream, and that soon enough he'd wake up in eternity, just another victim of a Fascist firing squad. Another name in the *generalísimo*'s fat docket of holy martyrs, ha.

10

OH SPAIN. BLOODY Spain. Bloody Franco. How many years was it now? He has Parkinson's disease. He has thrombophlebitis. He has stomach ulcers and a weak heart, he can't stop trembling and his mind wanders. He is eighty-four years old and I should know, I'm getting there myself. How he's kept his hand on the levers of power as long as he has while his body inexorably disintegrates, as though a just fate were taking reprisal for all the evil he's done in the world, it's beyond me.

I didn't see him for several days. I dared to hope he'd fled away on his astral journey, or whatever it bloody was – and himself not even dead yet, apparently. But I'd pulled the wing chair to the side of the bed, just in case, you see, because I wanted to know what it was he *wanted*, and one night, suddenly, I awoke – and there he was. There he was, sitting in shadow, my pitiful little *generalísimo*, same uniform as before and it smelled no better. Where had he come from, the morgue?

– *El anticoagulante que tomó complica mis úlceras*—

He spoke rapidly and he was hoarse, sibilant, almost inaudible as he sat there with his rusty medals glinting dully in the gloom. I think he was telling me that the drugs he took for his thrombosis didn't agree with those he took for his ulcers. I drove an ambulance once. I understand these things. He picked at the cuff of his tunic where the braid was coming unstitched and gazed at me from sad, tired, watery, long-lashed eyes, then all at once he groaned, and whispered the word *insoportable*. He seemed so small, nodding over his little paunch, and his mouth hanging open, dribbling, as though he had no idea who I was, or where he was, or what he was supposed to be doing here. He closed his eyes. He fell into a doze.

He was rather a feminine little thing, it occurred to me, not for the first time, and I remembered that his fellow officers used to call him 'Miss Canary Islands'. It wasn't hard to see why, given the silverware that hung about his person, and just a touch of blusher, a little kohl around the eyes. But the Canary Islands, this was all before he airlifted his Army of Africa across the Straits of Gibraltar and the killing began. And here he was now, old, and sick, and shivering, and I was about to get out of bed and find him a blanket when I heard a faint knock on the door.

– Papá?

His head came up and he stared at me. They said it was Ramón who'd fathered his daughter with Doña

45

Carmen, Ramón Franco, that is, the wild brother, the handsome one, the famous aviator—

– I'm all right, Gilly, I called softly, my eyes upon my visitor.

– *Me debes una disculpa*—

What!

– Can we come in?

– No, don't come in.

It would have made no difference, he was gone. *¿Me debes una disculpa?* You owe me an apology? Gilly opened the door. Finty was with her, also Dolores López. The three of them stood in the doorway and there I was, startled and alone, sitting up in bed in my pyjamas like a schoolboy. Dolores López, how inscrutable she was, yes, but so very *complicit*, I felt it then. Complicit.

– Papá, said Gilly, we heard voices. What *is* that *smell*?

11

OH, BUT WE protect our insularity as best we can – I speak for myself now – but a man who drove an ambulance in Spain, as I did, and was in Madrid during the bombing, and later at the Battle of the Jarama River, and elsewhere, and who faced a firing squad – he will be *storied* whether he likes it or not. It is widely believed that I was tortured. I was, but not in a manner you would recognise as such. I was also sentenced to death, but spared, again inadvertently.

But none of this was relevant to my immediate predicament. What *is* that *smell*? Was I to tell her the truth? Would this be remembered as the moment when I declared my so-called delusion without reserve, yes, without obfuscation of any kind? Or would I perhaps say: oh, *that* smell – and tell them a story of tracking manure upstairs from the garden?

– That smell, dear Gilly, is the stench of a monster.

– What sort of a monster?

– A moral monster.

– Bearing the likeness of a man?

– Yes.

– Oh, Pa, not again.

There. You see? I would not be taken seriously. Gilly went to the window and twitched back the curtain, as though she might glimpse this monster of mine flapping off into the night sky like a bat. My bedroom overlooks the garden, and at that time of night little can be seen but for the blackness of the trees, and only the faintest glow from the city beyond. It was a warm night, the window was open, and the earth was pungent, malodorous, for my garden – and this had come as a recent and most unwelcome shock to me – was starting to mildew and rot. It was suffering some kind of infestation, and not one I had seen before.

– It's rather a bad smell, isn't it? Gilly then said, with her back to me still.

I began to tell her it was the Spanish jasmine.

– It's Franco, isn't it, Pa? Isn't that what you think?

Moment of truth, you might say.

– The *generalísimo*, yes.

Give him his rank, at least. At this point Dolores López left the room and we heard her stamping off down the stairs. *Blam! – Splat! – Blam!* That man's name could never be spoken in her presence. Meanwhile Finty moved to the back of the room, by the window, on her black stick, and sat on the upright chair. And there she

48

remained. Eyes downcast, hands folded on top of her stick, while Gilly paced and fretted.

– But an apparition all the same, she said.

It had given me no particular pleasure to keep this knowledge from her. Now I felt it as a relief to allow her to take up some part of the burden, by which I mean, to acknowledge the predicament in which I found myself.

– What are we to do, Pa?

But oh, how my poor heart did lift and sing when I heard these words – what are *we* to do, *we*! After a few seconds I was able to reply.

– What do you suggest we do, Gilly?

She gazed at me.

– Pa, are you crying?

– I'm allergic to something in the garden. Close the window, dear, it's the night stock.

She sat on the bed and took my hands. She continued to gaze at me with some seriousness, frowning.

– Has he died? she said.

– No. We'd have heard.

Oh, enough. It was high time, I thought, that I got out of bed and stopped behaving like an invalid, it was not I who malingered in decrepitude! I was young once. Hard to believe, I know, but there were many of us then who realised that the world was going all to hell, and that what we wanted was to *stop fascism*, and one had to do something. Like *go to Spain*. Like *support the Popular Front*. Comrade. Yes, so I'd volunteered for the International Brigades. And I'd crossed the Channel on a ferry, with some young men like myself, and we'd slept on hard benches in the third-class lounge, and in the morning boarded a noisy, crowded train for Paris—

All this and more I told Gilly. She listened patiently. She'd heard it before.

– Go on, Pa, she said.

So I told her again about Marseille, and the Spanish fishing boat, and how we attracted the attention of an Italian warship, and when they saw us they changed course and we had to turn back, oh, and how we arrived in Madrid in convoy one night, in the middle of an air raid, and how I met Doc Roscoe, who taught me to transfuse blood, clean a septic wound—

But it was strange, I thought later, that Gilly should ask me if he was dead, Franco, I mean. Though no more strange I suppose than me seeing him from the top of a bus, or in the garden, or at my bedside, where he'd been growing more at ease lately, and talking a little. Or mumbling, rather: the hiss of dry lips that could never be moistened, ha. He whispers to me about the great Moroccan campaigns, how he and Luis Carrero put down the rising of Abd el-Krim, and how the priests started calling him the reincarnation of the Cid, and he became the youngest general in Europe at the age of thirty-three.

How old men do like to preen.

He was always at heart an *africanista*, he confided to me. *¿Africanista?* More like the ghoul in my bedroom, I thought, when he whispered his secrets in a wheezing *gallego* that convinced me all the more of his utter geriatric decadence. He told me he was born to rule,

that his own destiny and that of Spain were insepar-
able, and that the saints blessed his endeavours – which
were shortly, surely, to come to an end, I thought. No,
but this old boy, this figure of *pathos in extremis*, his days
were numbered, if not quite over yet. And while there
was life in him still, I thought, I may as well try and
understand what kind of a monster he was. The world
would surely thank me for that.

Or perhaps not. The world might prefer I keep it to
myself. As for owing him an apology: if anybody owed
someone an apology—

I got out of bed and slipped into my dressing gown
then sat in the gold-threaded wing chair the old ghoul
had just recently vacated. I lifted my eyebrows as though
to say, is all well? – as Finty glanced up and rearranged
her fingers on her stick, then once more looked at the
floor. Gilly was leaning against the wardrobe now, her
hands behind her back as she watched me, still frowning,
and somewhere in Cleaver Square a dog was barking
and I thought that wicked cat Henry Threshold might
be out. I indicated the decanter.

– I suppose so, said Gilly.

I poured us each a small sherry. Finty lifted a finger,
no thanks. I tapped my glass.

– To the revolution.

Gilly nodded wanly. Old joke.

– Is he dead? I said. Well, no.

– I didn't think so. And how many times have you
seen him?

I told her.

– But he is going to die, she said.

– One assumes.

– And you don't want to see someone about this, Pa?

I did not, and now she understood why, or so I hoped.

– And when he does die? she said.

The question hung there in the silence, as the city slept, and somewhere in Madrid the *generalísimo*, scourge of Spain, lay dying in an ancient royal palace full of Goyas, but somehow sustained living contact with a man whose life he had touched some forty years before. I had at least the comfort of Gilly's support now, and Finty's also, I think. And despite the dying man's smell in my room I believe I had convinced my daughter of my own compos mentis, I mean that I wasn't imagining it, it was no apparition, and I didn't need to *see someone*. What of course mattered now was that Gilly keep all this to herself. It wouldn't do if others were to hear that old Francis McNulty had got himself unhinged by a delusion. For yes, we protect our insularity as best we can, but people are so very ready to assume the worst.

– Gilly, I said.

– Pa.

– This must remain our secret. You cannot tell Percy.

– Oh, Pa, of course not. What did you think?

12

GILLY, YOU SEE, is a civil servant. She works in Whitehall, the Foreign Office, King Charles Street, Department of Southern Europe and North Africa. I have been there. You climb a splendid staircase then go down a long corridor and into a large room with a high ceiling and tall windows. It is loud with clattering typewriters, *ding! ding!* – wheezing teleprinters and men and women of all ages talking on telephones. Gilly has a small office on the same floor and her work involves reading heaps of buff-coloured government folders containing encoded cables from various of our embassies but mainly Madrid. What a thing it is! She emends them, she initials them, dates them and sends them on. Her immediate superior is an exhausted man of fifty called Edmund Mee, who yearns still for his lost consulate in British Honduras. But the point is that Gilly knows how to keep a secret, it is what she does for a

53

living: she keeps government secrets. So my secret – and what other secret, at this late stage, would concern me? – was safe with her.

But I am worried. For all that Gilly has apparently accepted my explanation as to the smell in my room, I fear she is not truly convinced. She suspects I am losing my mind. The nightmares concern her considerably. But what is it she fears exactly? That I will start neglecting myself, ignore personal hygiene, again leave the house in my pyjamas at dead of night? You do see old men in London who've let themselves go, they look like tramps, wild-eyed, and hallucinating madly. They hang around the National Gallery, or the Old Bailey, their trousers held up with bits of string. Some of them sit in the House of Lords.

Gillian seems to think this will happen to me. Well, of course it won't, the House of Lords? I spit upon the House of Lords! When I go past the House of Lords on the bus? Out with the hanky! But she's at least got me off the gin, after that nasty fall I took in March. But I do sometimes think, what is it I'm good for now? Finish those damn poems, if I can lay my hands on them. And get that damn *ghoul* out of the house.

It's too much. At times I doubt I'll make it through the winter. Oh but life is not without its distractions, I suppose. Often these days I will step across the square to the Earl of Rochester before lunch and have a drink with young Hugh Supple, he of the *Manchester Guardian*, who now tells me he'd like to write a long piece about my experiences in Spain, by way of giving context to the poetry. This is heartening, for I have much to say, and in Hugh Supple I have found a most sympathetic amanuensis, and I even think that at times he flirts with me, which is absurd on its face but not unwelcome for all that. More than once Finty has had to come over and haul me out, and when she does I murmur something droll and go off like a good boy.

But on occasion, yes, I do find my spirit all atremble. He may have departed for good, or not, I could not say for sure, for I have more pressing worries. Yes. I feel at times – and I find this extraordinarily difficult to admit – I confess I feel that my sanity is under threat. Yes. I am having moments of uncertainty as to where I am, and what I am supposed to be doing there. I have spells of apathy, and trouble buttoning my clothes. And how very difficult it is getting up in the morning! – the rising, the dressing, the shaving. The moving of the bowels. At times my balance is all to hell: I seem to have to cling to things! I conceal all this from Gilly, of course, but now there is Finty in the house as well, and of course the sharp-eyed Dolores López who misses nothing. She hates the *generalísimo* as I do, if not more so, and may have been planning some action against him. And would I try to prevent her? *I think not!*

But what I dread now is not this ghoul but something far worse: the curtailment of my freedom of movement. Yes. For I am aware that it happens to elderly persons like myself who, having once displayed some slight confusion on rising from an armchair – for instance – become thereafter not only closely watched, but prevented from going alone into the West End at night, or to Smithfield Market, or even across Cleaver Square for a pleasantly restorative gin and tonic in the saloon bar of the Earl of Rochester, perhaps with a young friend like Hugh Supple. It hasn't come to that yet. But it might.

What I most fear is that they think me frail. Frail! It is a word I *hate*. Call me mad, if you must; but never frail.

And there is that other anxiety, of course. It concerns Gillian and her future, which is very much my own. In a way it is flatly opposed to the problem of surveillance and control, for what worries me now is abandonment. I don't wish to give the wrong impression here lest I sound like one of those tedious creatures of the popular imagination, the ageing poet in need of care in his dotage. I would remind the reader, I would remind the reader – oh, I forget what I would remind the reader—

And then one night—

No! Not yet! Before any of that happened there were developments with regard to Gilly. You will remember that she had detected a smell. What *is* that *smell*, Pa? she'd said, and I had hidden nothing from her, the fact that it was a moral monster, in the form of a desert ghoul, which I have come to believe is the physical embodiment of the Principle of Ethical Disintegration. Yes. Which is – and I do not say this lightly – invariably triggered by the savagery of war. This is my conclusion. So it is no apparition, which I think Gilly now accepts. And I hope she will also accept that I am in fact proceeding with the matter in the only way possible, that is, without any flailing out at the thing, which would surely fail. No, wait it out. We are at least *entrenched*, and the ghoul is dying – its blood cells lack cytoplasm, for God's sake! Why it happened upon this house, and this veteran of his bloody civil war, well, that is the mystery.

Ghoul. Yes. Not a word I use carelessly, very few words I use carelessly, I was once a poet. I can't write it now, poetry. Those rivers of imagery that, oh! – that once swept through my imagination like ancient mighty waters in flood? All long since departed. But yes, I am coming to believe my night visitor is some kind of spirit, or ghoul, because in the morning I awaken exhausted, as though I've been handled really rather roughly through the hours of darkness. I feel estranged from the events of the night, uncertain as to the nature of the experience in which I have participated, and for which I have no explanation, for I don't think I've been dreaming.

And to live in the world and carry within myself this what – mystery – this knot of fog – impossible to articulate without arousing suspicion that I am, yes, going mad – this is now my task, as I see it. And meanwhile I tend my garden, such as it is, infested and rotting precisely because of the presence of this ghoul, yes, and some plants dead already.

And then one night—

13

B UT NO, THERE was no such night. For all at once his visits ceased. It is September already, and with some caution I consider the possibility that he's left – for good. Just as well I was so circumspect with Gilly. Certainly there is much to occupy him in Madrid, despite his advancing senility, as Percy Gauss has been telling me. Two death sentences have been handed down, Basques, of course, then a third. Then eight more. Some thought them to be in reprisal for the murder of Carrero Blanco, blown to bits by *los vascos* after attending Mass in Madrid.

There was also the execution by *garrote vil* of that young Catalan anarchist, Salvador Puig Antich. I am still unable to speak of him.

And the world is in uproar. Huge demonstrations, attacks on Spanish embassies. Senior diplomats recalled. Even the Pope has woken up and appealed for clemency.

He ignores them all. He is seen to be infirm, not to say profoundly psychologically incapacitated. One night five of the death sentences were confirmed. The condemned men were shot at dawn. This was widely regarded at least in the *Manchester Guardian* as a gesture not of the regime's strength, rather of its decay, also of its susceptibility to the influence of the parties of the far right. It is apparent to the world as never before that not only has Spain failed to become a modern state, but that it has slipped ever deeper into a new Dark Age, with a new inquisitorial pogrom; and that this will be his legacy.

All this I explained to Gilly. I've told her she doesn't have to look after me. Dolores López is here and she can see to my needs, such as they are, but Gilly insists. She seems to think I'm on my last legs, and that without her own watchful eye I will soon collapse into madness and infirmity. Ha. But perhaps now that she has accepted Percy Gauss this will change, and she will reclaim the life she once had, before she moved back to Cleaver Square to *keep an eye on me*, as she says. No eye needed, I cry, but does she listen?

But then had come the *verdugo* nightmare and all the disruption it caused, and after that the malodorous memories, up they'd bubbled as though from the very toilets of hell, and all this too I explained to Gilly although not in detail, trusting her to put the rest together by herself. She'd gazed at me, nodding, and the horror I believe was clear to her – and, I think, I *think* – she understood. She asked only one question.

– But is there any pattern to it, Pa?

I asked her what she meant.

– I mean as to when he comes? When he appears, I mean? Do you have a feeling about it? Do you ever think, I'll be seeing him tonight, and then you do?

There were aspects of the matter which I didn't yet wish to discuss with her. I said this.

– But you must tell me, she cried. I can't help you otherwise, well, can I?

– You're already helping me considerably, dear.

– Yes but if you won't tell me everything I'll always have one hand tied behind my back. You do see that?

We were out on the terrace, well, I call it a terrace, more of a balcony really, over the backyard. Two or three wicker chairs, a table, nice for drinks because you can look out over the garden. It was Sunday, early evening. Finty had gone with Dolores López to the six o'clock Mass at St Francis Xavier. A good Catholic all her life, Finty, as was Gilly, rosary in the handbag, crucifix over the bed, all that nonsense. But a warm, damp, quiet evening after a day of light rain and mist. A good day for me, for in the absence of the *generalísimo* I was rallying, meaning fewer aches and pains than usual, my balance a little improved, and just a very few slight traces of the depression that affects me in the late afternoon, usually, and persists into the evening, when only the release that comes with sleep subdues it, if no nightmare intrudes.

It is worse if I drink a glass or two of sherry at lunchtime, and so I have had to forgo that small pleasure, as I've had to forgo so many others. For oh dear, it is a

60

spartan business, this growing old, this cleaving to life, because it demands that you jettison so much that once had been the very zest and pith of life, and why? So that life, pithless, and *sans zest*, may continue, and the flesh, oh, the flesh, the sins of the flesh – they are as motes in a fading sunbeam. And how I do miss them.

Yes.

But still I have Whitman. And Yeats. And Poe and Swinburne. And Melville. And Goya. Goya, yes, greatest of all the Spanish painters, to my taste, and I like to visit him in the National Gallery, and in particular his *Lámpara del Diablo*, otherwise known as *The Bewitched Man*. It depicts some poor fellow in the depths of the night attempting to keep his lamp alight, for being bewitched, if he should let the lamp die then his soul will be forfeit to the Devil.

I feel I share his fate, perhaps we all do. Allow the light to die and your soul is forfeit. But what Gilly doesn't know, and I am convinced she must never know it, is that he doesn't just *appear*, not as he did in the latter part of the summer, and that I do have something to do with it. He takes my mind off my predicament. He tells me I owe him an apology. And I find it hard to explain even to myself how that first horror has faded into a sort of resignation, which has shaded into – compassion, can I call it? – but still, oddly, with no less alertness as to the creature's manifest corruption. Gilly thinks I am deluded, and I deny it. But perhaps it is my delusion to think that I might come to understand the creature, *and live with it.*

How to explain that? I will tell you. He reminds me of someone. He reminds me of my father. Daddy. That man taught me the bitter lesson that a tyrant without power is a very pitiful creature indeed. But of course – no less vicious for that. Ethical disintegration, once begun, it knows no bounds.

– Pa, what aren't you telling me?

She had turned in her chair, a bleached wicker job with curved wooden arms and legs, one of a half-dozen I'd got from an old gent who'd come to the door one day, and whom I'd invited in for a cup of tea.

– I'm telling you everything.

– But not what you think.

– I think this man is about to die.

– And you feel sorry for him.

– Darling, I am human. It's easy to forget, I know. I forget it myself at times.

– Oh shut up. This thing isn't human, it's a bloody delusion. Nobody else has seen it.

Her anger came as a shock. I didn't mention Dolores López. She's seen it.

– It is not a delusion, Gilly. It is a ghoul, if you must know. A desert ghoul. A ghoul of the waste. If you must know. I thought we'd been through all this.

But she appeared not to have heard me. Yes, I'd thought she understood. I'd thought she was on my side now. More fool me. She was sitting forward, head up, elbows high and arched with her hands gripped tight to the arms of the chair, and staring straight into the garden, which seemed more full of threat than usual that day. Her pale lovely face was bathed in creeping shadow, and in profile, in the quickening dusk, she was aquiline – yes – and no mere sparrow, no little *pecker*, my Gilly, but a bird of prey, osprey, kite! Then her eyes were upon me, sideways, flashing.

– A *ghoul of the waste*? Oh, come on, Pa!

– What about the smell? I cried.

– I think you tracked it in from the garden.

This provoked in me a bitter snort, for it was precisely the explanation I'd planned to give her myself, only I chose instead to tell her the truth. She was fully turned towards me now, and she was wearing that delicate pale blue cardigan of soft cashmere thrown carelessly over her shoulders with the sleeves hanging empty so she appeared hooded, angry, an avenging angel – my raptor! Her hair was loose, and one perfect white hand lay upon the other on the arm of the chair.

– How nice you look, I murmured.

– You know what I suggest? she said.

– Tell me.

– That you see someone, yes, Pa, don't groan like that, because now I do have someone specific in mind and I've talked to her about you. Can I tell you?

I rose to my feet, not without some difficulty, and as I turned to go back inside I flung a glance at her and caught the expression on her fierce hawk face. Anger, yes, and resolution. Oh, I would have to keep my wits about me now. She'd talked to some shrink about me. But I was damned if I'd let her get away with any of *that*. What, an old-age psychiatrist? They get called in when you start to think people are stealing your things. People are, of course, stealing my things, but it's not because I'm mad, it's because I've got so many things worth stealing. There's a batch of unfinished poems which has disappeared from my desk, and I'd very much like to *have them back*!

I remember what I would remind the reader. I would remind the reader that I went to Spain in 1936, where I drove an ambulance during the siege of Madrid and elsewhere. I have married a number of women (two), loved a number of – other people – (twenty-two), written a number of slim volumes of modern Romantic poetry published by reputable small presses like Hyperbole, and sustained this old house in Cleaver Square where I have raised a fine garden (now dying), and also a daughter. And when I wish to go to the West End alone at night, to attend, let us say, a concert of classical music, Schubert perhaps, *Death and the Maiden* – I go.

So let there be no more of this clucking and wheedling. *Oh, Pa, are you sure?* Or: *Oh, Francis, is this really a good idea?* Let me be clear. I am always sure, and it is always a good idea.

14

KEEP MY WITS about me, easier said than done in this house. One last *vastation* – for this I have learned is the proper term, it's Swedenborg – one in particular you have to hear about, can you bear it? I had become accustomed to being awoken in the silence in the small hours to find in the glow of my night light the old ghoul seated in the wing chair with his head thrown back and his mouth open, his halting breath fouling the air and his little lady's hands twitching and scratching at the upholstery as he pulled out the stuffing. When he turned an inch or two towards me I saw what I liked to believe was a flicker of gratitude, the understanding, I mean, that he was no longer alone in the darkness – his gratitude that a fellow pilgrim had appeared to keep vigil with him through the long watches of the night, when the mind is most actively fearful of death. It's how I saw my poor father out, yes, to the strains of

Prokofiev, Violin Sonata No. 1, which he loved. One of the saddest nights of my life.

The thing in the wing chair speaks, but only because it is his habit to speak in the presence of an audience. Which does not mean he requires conversation. Very rarely can I elicit a response from him, and only if I persist do I ever catch a murmur from the ruins, as it were, all that is left, I mean, of a heart that burned once with hatred and fury, and ambition, and self-love, and terror, too, of the enemy within – within Spain, within his own party, within himself.

But all gone now, disappeared, just a wasted husk, like an old flamenco dancer bent over his stick, although the habit of passion does still linger, faintly, and to my soft insistent enquiries – why the terror? The torture? Why was the Principle of Ethical Disintegration permitted to flourish with such vigour, why did they all have to die? And why did they have to die even when the war was won, and your power secure, and no rival on the horizon as far as the eye could see? When it could have been over months before? But no, you wanted not just to win but to annihilate *every single last one of them* – *todos aniquilados* – your enemies, I mean, real and imagined.

But if you had not – I said – had you desisted – had the quality of mercy found some *fingernail* of soil on which might fall a mere *droplet* of the precious fluid – in all the arid nothingness of your being – then Doc Roscoe would be alive today. I believe this. His was a careless death, and him a man towards whom you had once recognised a moral debt. How careless you were with all our lives, and this you'd learned in the North African campaigns, when life was so very cheap indeed. I said, so how did you decide which death sentences to approve, when the lists were put before you?

A shrug. You said you never had any doubt as to the guilt of your enemies.

Nor was it over yet. Political arrests continue. Summary trials. The Angelus bell clanging in the night, volleys of gunfire, and the endless shovelling of nameless bodies into bottomless pits, yes, even and including Federico García Lorca, your greatest living poet, as was, you *filis-teo!* And you, meanwhile, vain foolish man, being driven around the streets of Madrid in an open Mercedes-Benz, all sashed and bemedalled, a touch of lipstick, glossy fingernails in calfskin gloves, I can see you now. And delirious crowds, all screaming, *¡Viva Franco! ¡Viva Franco! Franco, Franco, Franco—*

It gets me nowhere. He's heard enough. He's heard nothing at all. He's gone. I sit in my malodorous bedroom – *my* bedroom? – *mine?* – I think not. I think of the men who came back and who gather in the Bull in Smithfield Market one Monday every month, when the first topic of conversation is, always: is he still alive? Is he dead yet?

– Is he fuck.

This is Eddie Wargrave speaking.

We drink to his death in fervent hope it won't be pleasant or peaceful or quick. A moment's silence as with trembling hands we lift our glasses and one or two of the old boys in black berets lift the fist. I watch Sam

Ferber, him I knew at the Jarama River and later too. Forty years on, and some of them still active, by which I mean more active than I am now, not saying much I dare say, but then look at poor old Eddie Wargrave, not a young man when he arrived in Spain and crocked now, wheelchair, sticks, the works. But I watch him as he sits, frowning, and giving off the strong impression that if he detected the faintest whiff of fascism on a man's breath he'd be up out of that chair with his stick swinging, and God help the poor bastard on the other end of it. I also happen to know he has four cats. I talk to him about Henry Threshold and his face goes soft. He wants to know what I feed him. I tell him what Henry likes. Old Eddie nods.

– Got a photo, have you, Madge?

He has to change his spectacles for this operation. I remember when he helped us out, Doc and me, when we were overwhelmed at the Jarama after that 'at-all-costs-hold-your-ground' lunacy on Suicide Hill. Bloody terrifying, worst day of the war for many of us, those who survived it. Impossible for men to find cover, even dig a trench, and nobody had water. And so many on that hill killed or wounded you hardly knew where to start. Eddie and I were out there, bringing in those we thought might make it, and Doc working on three at once in the ambulance just over the ridge—

Now Eddie and I are peering at a photo of Henry Threshold, and it only takes one of us to say, that fucking hill, and we'd be back there, but neither of us does. It goes unsaid, well, what need? We both know we'd have done better to bring them in after dark but none of them could wait that long. It was half a mile to the ambulance – were we to leave them to die? Not with those monsters coming up the hill. There wasn't a grave they wouldn't desecrate.

Eddie and I say nothing about this. We saw horrors but why dwell on them? I have trouble enough with my dreams. It may be the same for Eddie, I don't ask. We talk about our cats instead, and it's a joy to see the crust of ill temper on the face of an old man whose world has become incomprehensible to him, as it breaks up – not unlike an iceberg, it occurs to me, thawing in springtime – at the sight of an impassive, indifferent, supercilious cat. And we think about God knows what, to each his own, although for me it's the streets of Barcelona after the so-called repatriation agreement, when we were on our way home. I mean the parade down the Ramblas, thousands of us, remnants of the International Brigades, in some sort of military order but out of step because nobody ever really taught us how to march.

The good people of Barcelona didn't care. They'd turned out in their tens of thousands, oh, on their balconies and rooftops, running along beside us, throwing flowers, shouting *¡Viva!* And La Pasionaria is on the reviewing stand, shaking the fist and shouting that we could go proudly because we were history, we were legend, we were heroes of democracy and would not be forgotten! But all I could think of was Doc—

Gilly believes I spend too much time thinking about this stuff but I ask her, what stuff should I be thinking about? And there's Sally Manley at a small table with a glass of gin and a cigarette, or two cigarettes. Her white face, hollowed out and caved in now, she was a nurse, one of the best, and she's full of shrapnel from Brunete, where poor brave Julian Bell the poet died after taking shrapnel of his own while sheltering under his vehicle when the Germans came over. I sit down with her. Sal's lamp is guttering now and she knows it, and I think, dear God, I love this woman but it's not a thing you can say.

– I saw you in the paper, Madge, she says. How's the poetry?

I sometimes think her throat is paved with gravel. They used to call me Madge, I don't remember why.

– Slow, Sally, I say, I've got Finty in the house now.

She knows my sister. Ghost of a smile, and then she starts coughing.

– No rest then, she says eventually, when she's got another fag on the go.

– Not for the wicked.

The thing in the bed snorts. I sit gasping in the wing chair. I cannot imagine how I will ever sleep in that bed again.

15

I'D BEEN HALF wakened from some kind of a fever dream and lay there conscious, but dimly, that I was not alone in the bed. And that he or it, or whatever it was, was breathing on the back of my neck, and then I heard broken gasps, sudden choked snorts, and felt him pushing at me, and drowsy though I was, for I'd taken another pill—

– Daddy? I whispered.

Suddenly I was wide awake. I felt him stir, and I turned with dread, with terror, even, to look over my shoulder, and in the gloom appeared from under the bedclothes a pair of fat, short-fingered hands which all at once reached for my face and that was it for me, I was out of that bed, my flesh alive and all aquiver with horror at the *presence* of the thing, and I collapsed in the wing chair, gasping for breath, and stared at what it was that was in my bed but had now like a crab withdrawn back under the blankets, and I knew I wouldn't be able to get into that bed again, ever. It had been my parents' bed, and then after Mummy ran off with Roger Dixon it was *his* bed, Daddy's bed, the bed in which he'd died, and it was not lost on me that we had changed places, he and I, that he was now the host, and I the ghost—

Quietly then I left the bedroom that was no longer mine, and climbed the attic stairs. My dressing gown hung open over my pyjamas, as moonlight streamed in through the high window and the boards creaked beneath me, but I knew she wouldn't wake up, Finty could sleep through anything. The attic runs the width of the house and has a sloping ceiling and two dormer windows. Exposed beams above and bare boards underfoot, and a wardrobe at one end, also an armchair. Spartan, say the least. Beside the bed, which is a boy's dorm-room job with bad springs and a hard mattress, there is a table on which stands a small lamp, some paperbacks and a missal. On the wall above the bed among various of Finty's seascapes hangs a black crucifix with the body of the Christ in yellow ivory attached. Finty was fast asleep and I had not much trouble getting in beside her without disturbing her, despite the narrowness of the bed, she and I being both narrow ourselves. The window had been opened an inch or two and the curtains stirred in the breeze. There were sounds from the garden, a bird, a cat.

I folded my hands on my chest as though laid to rest in my coffin, and stared at the beams in the ceiling. All was still but for the very slight shifting of the curtains. I may have made some small involuntary movement and she turned towards me, and got herself up on an elbow, blinking at me.

– Oh, Francis, it's you. I couldn't think who it was, coming up the stairs and getting into bed with me.

– Go back to sleep, I whispered, I just needed company.

She yawned and I turned and lay with my back to her.

– The *generalísimo*, is it?

– It might have been Daddy.

Oh God. I just wanted to lie quiet. I was panting a little, and staring at the door now, thinking the bloody man would at any moment come lurching in upon us.

– Turn round, dear, I can't talk to your back.

So I did. Our faces were just a few inches apart. Now something screamed in the alley beyond the garden wall, fox, ghost. Some poor bastard being nailed to a cross.

– Pretty far gone, is it?

– Depends what you mean.

She touched my cheek. What she then murmured I could barely take in because for some damn reason I'd started to cry. The *generalísimo* was devoid of all human feeling and yet he wept often, but in me it is an excess of feeling rather than a lack. Finty got her arms around me then, and clasped my head to herself as best an arthritic old girl could manage, my cheek against her bony chest while I heaved and sobbed in her arms like a child, and let go whatever it was that was all stoppered up inside me. Then I grew calm and sat up in the bed. Finty had once been a mother to me. That was after Mummy left us and my poor father took to drink and became not responsible for his actions any more.

— If you don't know what that thing is, said Finty, then I most certainly don't.

This was encouraging, at least. It's not what Gilly would have said.

— I always thought you'd be the one to see a ghost, she then said, of all of us.

— You think I'm hysterical?

— I would say not. Receptive. Sensitive. Senile, of course.

Quiet cackle here.

— Sensitive to what?

— Everything. You're a poet, Francis.

— Do you remember what you told me the night Daddy died?

But if she remembered she didn't care to say so. I'd thought at the time she knew me better than I did myself, but of course it was so many years ago now. Later, when she'd gone to Mull, I would mourn her absence grievously. But by then of course everything had changed.

16

O<small>H</small> G<small>OD</small>. S<small>OME</small> days I feel like an ancient mariner and this is one of them. Unhand me, greybeard loon! – is how I imagine the reaction, should I seize upon some friendly soul so as to tell them my story. How has it come to this? Where once my life was populated with the living, now I seem to keep company only with ghosts and ghouls and the like. It has already been borne home to me that I've reached a stage in life where one loses one's friends and contemporaries at a quickening rate of attrition: a thinning of the ranks, yes. Old age a ceremony of losses, and old people a separate form of life. But I did not choose this! I wasn't asked! I do weep in the middle of the night, it is true, but the reason isn't so hard to find. Self-pity. Shame. The suspicion that I'm haunted not by the *generalísimo* but by my own reflection, I mean that the thing isn't out there, it's in here. I know. Madness. The doppelgänger game, all too real. I hate it. But, you see, I'm losing Gilly, and why shouldn't I? Or rather, why shouldn't she cast me off? I am a liability to her. I am a liability to myself. One of these days I will fall over and break one bone or several and then where will we be? I can't bear to think about it. This body of mine gave much pleasure once and not only to myself. Now it's just a brittle arrangement of jointed sticks, and the world waits panting to trip me up, or knock me down – *snap!* – *crack!* – and Gilly knows it. I am an ancient mariner. I am an accident waiting to happen.

I am frail.

And the mind not much better. Gilly thinks I'm mad. She wants me to see a doctor, some old-age psychiatrist, well, perhaps I should, but what then? I dread to think. I hear heavy doors clang shut behind me, large keys thrust into big locks, and that's me done, banged up in a bin. Lost her mind, poor old Madge. Thinks she's haunted by a ghoul. Thinks it gets into her bed at night. She should be so lucky! Much laughter in the wings as I stand alone in an empty auditorium, in the middle of the stage, a single spotlight upon me as I turn this way and that, arms outstretched, palms spread wide, crying, why don't you help me, for God's sake – *I'm dying up here!*

Oh enough. What nonsense you do spew, you silly bloody old fool. Yes, unhand me, greybeard loon, no more of this mawk, thank you. I was in my study, looking for some poems, no more than usually distraught what with the various crosses I had to bear, not least being old and mad and haunted, when my sister tapped at the door then put her head in and told me to come into the sitting room for a minute.

– Darling, I'm trying to write, I said.

I seem to have been saying this to women my entire life. Actually it was a lie. Poems were missing. I'd gone through everything. I was particularly eager to locate them, there being some interest from a publisher. Yes, Hyperbole. Somebody's trying to revive it.

– Francis, just come into the sitting room.

There was a crisp tone now and I don't think I'd heard it for some time, possibly not since childhood, can this be right? It was clear she would brook no refusal. I rose to my feet but as I did so, she came back in again. She closed the door behind her and leaned against it, and gazed at me with an expression of ponderous gravity.

– Whatever is the matter? I cried. Why are you looking at me like that?

For a few seconds she said nothing. Henry was asleep in the armchair but now he awoke. He seemed to find the ambience disagreeable, and leapt lightly to the floor and padded across the carpet as Finty opened the door so he could slip away, having better things to do. As did I.

– Now, Francis, she said, you know how worried Gilly is.

– About what?

– You.

I sat down at my desk again, swivelled the chair round so I was facing her, and leaned back with my hands clasped behind my head. I smelled trouble.

– Go on.

77

– You're not yourself. You're drinking too much. You forget things. You can't even sleep in your own bed.

– If not myself, I began, and then fell silent.

– Come and meet someone.

At this she turned, and opened the door once more. I followed her across the hall, quietly protesting, telling her that nobody had to worry about me, everything was under control—

Then into the sitting room and a strange woman was there. She was tall, rather plump, nicely dressed, blonde hair tinted, bouffed, young woman of about fifty. She was standing by the fireplace with Gilly. She might be a dame, I thought, she had such presence. Like a successful London barrister, I thought, or a doctor—

Oh God. My heart sank. I froze.

– Francis, this is Mrs Doris Withers, said Gilly.

She will wither me, I thought.

– Mr McNulty, how do you do? she said in a firm, pleasant voice.

I shook her hand. How very fragrant she was, but all I could hear were the asylum gates clanging shut behind me.

– Mr McNulty, I understand you are thinking of selling your home?

I fled.

17

IT WASN'T RAINING exactly, nor even drizzling. It was misting. Through thin mist, then, I fled across Cleaver Square and straight into the Earl of Rochester. I stood heaving and panting at the counter of the saloon bar. Johnny, wiping his hands on a dishcloth, came to me at once.

– Morning, Francis.

– Gin and tonic, please, Johnny, large one.

Then came a familiar voice.

– Oh, Mr McNulty!

I turned. It was Hugh Supple, boy reporter from the *Manchester Guardian*. Was I glad to see him. Then the door swung open and there stood Gillian.

– Pa, she said.

I was on the back foot. I played for time. Holding my daughter's gaze I fumbled for coins in my trouser pocket and came up with a handful of silver and slapped it clattering onto the counter.

– I'm not ready for this, Gilly.

– Come now, please, Pa.

– This is out of order, Gilly, I have not been consulted—

– You have been consulted and you agreed. You have forgotten.

– No. No. You are wrong. Something like this I would have remembered.

My tone was one of astonished indignation.

– Papá. You have forgotten.

I was aware of Johnny hoving to with my gin. I pushed my silver towards him. Still gazing boldly, brazenly, even, at my daughter, I lifted to my parched lips the brimming tumbler, lots of ice in it, as I like it, the American way.

– Pa.

I had a good swallow then set the glass down. Hugh Supple, over by the window with a small glass of beer, had risen to his feet.

– I'm losing my patience, said Gilly.

– Very well.

I had another swallow. Christ alive! Johnny makes a stiff one! On my way out I shook Hugh's hand and told him I hoped we might meet later, and he said that was why he was here. Apparently we'd agreed to see each other today.

– Yes, I said. Very good idea.

I left the pub like a man leaving a courtroom in which he'd been found not guilty by reason of insanity and sent to Broadmoor. With my hands folded on my bowed head like a POW I followed my daughter across Cleaver Square. She turned.

– Now stop that right now! she said.

Once inside the house I walked straight into the sitting room, and as Doris Withers rose from the couch I apologised for my absence, saying I had an urgent letter to post.

– What can I do for you, Dr Withers? I said with my back to the fireplace, as though I were the master of the house, ha.

I then became aware that I was still in my writing clothes. The jacket was out at both elbows and a button hung from a single thread. The shirt collar was badly frayed, the trousers hadn't been cleaned in a decade, I was in bedroom slippers and without socks or tie. I am a poet! It is the life of the mind, of the spirit, which—

– It's Mrs Withers, not Doctor, I'm afraid, said the stately plump woman jovially. And I think it's more a question of what I can do for you.

Finty stood frowning by the French windows, then moved over to the couch, then got up and left the room. Gilly took up a position by the door, like a sentry. There followed a silence which might have been awkward but I felt no awkwardness at all. Trapped, perhaps. Shanghaied. Tricked, snagged. *Netted*, as though by a nimble-fingered butterfly collector in a meadow in Devon in June. Mrs Withers turned to Gilly, who was still leaning against the door, her eyes upon me, pale and fiery.

– Now, Pa, she said, can we talk about this calmly?

Later I would reflect on the conversation that followed and glimpse within it the first of the many and various attempts on Gilly's part to persuade me that I could no longer sustain life in Cleaver Square with Dolores López alone, and that my only recourse, if I wished to enjoy a settled and productive old age, was to move into Percy's house in Lord North Street. There I would have a garden, a study and a comfortable bedroom. She said she had never considered me to be so very attached to Cleaver Square, and that I was not a sentimental man, at heart.

– If not at heart—

– Pa, I know what's important to you. You need a room to write in. You need your books. And you need a garden. You can have all that in Percy's house.

– Yes, I said, and you've put your finger on it, darling. In *Percy's* house.

– Oh, Papá, Papá, what does that matter now?

You notice the *now*? Some freight it carried, that *now* – when your life is all but over, she meant, when you are *so* very close to the grave you can practically count the worms. I said this.

– I didn't mean that at all, she said.

– What did you mean?

And all this being conducted in front of Mrs Doris Withers, whom I now understood to be not an old-age psychiatrist but some lady come to appraise the value of my property. Gilly moved across to the sofa.

– Mrs Withers, as you can see, we've had a slight misunderstanding. I'm so sorry if we've wasted your time. May I be in touch with you tomorrow?

Mrs Doris Withers would already have taken in the size of the house, the French windows, the garden beyond, appraising it all. Gilly saw her out and returned to the sitting room. I was wandering around in some emotional disarray. I was feeling alarmed, and besieged. I had started to rub my hands together as a means of discharging the tension mounting in my psyche, yes, in my poet's psyche, which possesses a tough carapace, admittedly, highly resistant to intrusion as a general rule, but it is a complex organism for all that, and sensitive in the extreme.

– This is a bad shock, Gilly. A bad shock to spring on me out of the blue like this.

– We discussed it, Pa, she said wearily, standing before the mirror over the fireplace, gazing at herself and running her hands through her hair. She was wearing a narrow grey skirt with a maroon cardigan, and flat shoes. She asked me had I forgotten. I was standing with my back to the room, gazing out into the garden now, half expecting an appearance, or a manifestation, or a *vastation*, yes, in the middle of my wilting hydrangeas. It was the sort of occasion on which he might be expected to make an appearance. Without turning I said I had not been present at that discussion so how could I have forgotten it?

– Finty was present, said Gillian. She remembers it.

But Finty had slipped away. There are times in one's life when one has to cling to what one knows to be the truth while those around one insist one is wrong. One's decision to go to Spain being one. One said this.

Meanwhile Gilly was making for the door.

– Don't fetch her, I said, I know what she'll say. You want me to sell this house, I understand that. But, Gilly, you can't uproot me now!

The words were barely out of my mouth when I saw my error. I was speaking of myself as she had, as a man with one foot in the grave.

– How can you live here by yourself?

– I have Dolores López.

– Oh, Pa. You'll go mad.

I was about to turn back to the garden but I changed my mind, and asked Gilly with some anger how she could have brought that woman into the house without telling me, that Mrs Withers.

– It is a legal matter, Pa.

– A *legal matter*?

– If we are to sell the house she needs to see the deeds. You have them. You also have the power of attorney.

– Of course I do. And I intend to exercise it.

Gilly slumped into the red armchair and covered her face with her hands. She groaned. I thought: Where are the bloody deeds? I had no idea! At that moment Finty came back into the room. I turned back to the French windows and stared at the garden. Still no sign of the *generalísimo*.

– Pa, said Gilly, I have a question. Why *did* you go to Spain? I have never understood that.

– I went to Spain, I said, to become a member of the human race.

– Did it work?

– Up to a point.

– What point was that?

Then the door from the basement into the yard creaked open. I saw Dolores López come out shouldering a bulky Indian rug, which she then flung over the clothes line. Henry appeared from nowhere and leapt onto the wall behind the silver birch. Dolores López rolled her sleeves up and began vigorously to beat the rug. Dust rose into the damp autumnal air. She was really whacking it. Henry was fascinated.

– Where were we?

– You went to Spain to join the human race and it worked, up to a point. To what point?

– Do you know what Spain was then, Gilly? One enormous hospital.

– You drove an ambulance, Pa.

Did she have any idea?

– I drove an ambulance, a lorry, a motorbike, anything on wheels to get an injured man to a doctor. I even carried stretchers, extremely dangerous work, Gilly. I was an orderly. Sometimes I scrubbed for Doc Roscoe, American surgeon. That means I assisted him with sterilised equipment while he operated, and often he operated for fourteen hours at a stretch without a break. Why am I telling you all this?

– I don't know, Pa. You brought it up.

– No, Gilly, you did. Ambulances, lorries, whatever. There was a boy, I remember, a medical student, Felipe, from Madrid, and it was his job to keep the vehicles running. One morning they wouldn't start because of the cold. He should have remembered to drain the tanks, you see, or kept them warm with a Primus.

– So what happened, Pa?

– They took him out behind a wall and made him kneel down with his face against it and then they shot him in the back of the head.

Gilly's hands flew to her mouth.

– Oh good God. Why?

– Sabotage, that's what they thought.

– No.

– Oh yes. And these were Republicans, our own people. There was a rich man, a philanthropist—

– Pa—

– They buried him alive—

– Pa, enough!

Finty was leaning against the sideboard and Gilly was still in the red armchair. She shook her head. There was nothing more to say. I left the sitting room and slowly climbed the stairs. I lay down on my bed with my hands crossed on my chest and allowed my breathing to subside. I didn't want to think about Felipe. Why did I say all that? I could feel the beginnings of a headache. It was the gin. I'd had no breakfast.

18

S IR PERCY GAUSS was twenty years older than Gilly. I had met him on a number of occasions when he'd come to Cleaver Square for drinks, and I had formed a tentative affection for the man despite his politics. He looked to be in reasonable health. He had little colour in his cheeks but he could rise from an armchair without apparent difficulty. He was an inch or two taller than me but just as thin and he wore a habitual expression of mild ironic bemusement on his face, not without a splash of malice; attractive in a man, I've always thought. He was something important in the Foreign Office, and a senior member of the Conservative Party. If they ever got back into power, Gilly said, he might have a Cabinet post.

Percy had invited me to lunch and I suspected this was at Gilly's prompting. I think it must have occurred soon after Mrs Doris Withers came to the house, and that was late August or early September perhaps, who can remember these things? It was when I first saw mildew on the asters, a most distressing development. I had never heard of asters suffering from mildew. Such delicate little things they appear, but they are really rather tough. Breaks your heart. No question as to where responsibility lay for that act of vandalism.

I was to join him at his club in St James's. Now given my well-known unease, say the least, in any bastion of privilege or tradition, it was with some relief that I saw the man himself approaching me across the lobby when I entered, himself in a pinstriped suit and big black shoes – *clang! splat! clang!* – and grinning, with his arms extended.

– Francis – very good to see you, my dear. Now come on up to the bar, you probably want a drink.

– Of course, I murmured, and allowed this tall, pale, charming fellow to sweep me up the broad curving staircase of this august, marbled old joint in which Englishmen for centuries had sat contemplating their wealth and status and that of their neighbours. I was in my pale green tweed suit over a maroon shirt and a spotted red cravat, and on my feet a pair of hand-sewn suede brogues, pale ochre, of which I'm rather proud. I was feeling a little shaky for as I say it was only a few days since I'd found Mrs Doris Withers in my sitting room saying she understood I wished to sell my home. The prospect of a serious drink was welcome.

We entered a large dark-panelled saloon bar where gentlemen in ancient leather armchairs and chesterfields emitted a low collective susurrus like a community of ageing Californian elephant seals, mingled with barks of whiskered Tory walrus. There was a broad, high fireplace, roaring now, it being a cool day, and portraits in oil of distinguished members from generations past, hanging judges, land robbers, slave traders. It's useful to get a look at the enemy from time to time. We passed through into the dining room and, once seated, ordered drinks, a Gordon's martini for me, for him a Scotch.

– So, Francis.

– Percy.

We talked of this and that until our drinks arrived. We saluted each other with a tip of the head. Then, ah! – the first glorious shock of a good gin martini, like a fat stick of gelignite up the arse, pardon my French, and it bucked me considerably. As you may imagine.

– Now, Francis, he said.

He seemed to be squaring himself, organising for the assault, and I attempted to focus what slender resources I still possessed. This man after all intended to marry Gillian. Once she became his, she would no longer be mine, and he would take her away. Finty would return to the Isle of Mull and I would be alone. I didn't count Dolores López – perhaps I should have done. If I spoke better Spanish, or if she spoke better English. Or any English at all, ha. She does speak English but prefers not to, I don't know why. Pride. So yes, the future, with McNulty abandoned – old, mad, haunted – and alone. The threat this man presented, small wonder I was shaky.

– This is a little delicate, Percy Gauss began.

Here it comes, I thought.

– As you know, Francis, Gilly and I are to be married.

Oh, get on with it, I thought.

– I would wish her to live with me, in my house.

I'd heard about this house. Big place in Westminster. Lord North Street, or Smith Square, I didn't remember exactly.

– We would like you to live with us.

– Live with you! I cried.

Heads turned. Percy appeared wryly amused. Some confusion in the elderly party, clearly.

– Is that so very daunting a prospect?

– I didn't expect it.

I laid a finger or two on the stem of my martini glass, as though to defer my response with a bit of business in the cocktail department, but I didn't actually lift the thing to my lips. I have not had a clear head since about 1956, Suez Crisis, but whatever clarity did remain, I needed it now. I summoned it. Then the words were out of my mouth.

– What, leave Cleaver Square?

He gazed at me with his eyebrows lifted. He didn't need to say anything. I'd seen off Mrs Doris Withers, so I thought, and assumed that all I now had to fear was Gilly's departure.

– Leave Cleaver Square? I said again.

Later it occurred to me that it wasn't abandonment I should have been worried about at all, but internment. Bondage. Captivity. Oh, but it was far too late for any of that, surely he realised it? He was peering at the table and pushing the salt cellar up against the mustard as though playing condiment chess with himself. His eyes lifted.

– You are thinking of your garden, of course.

Was I thinking of my garden? I was now. And when I thought of my garden I thought about *blight*, and the causes of *blight*.

– I can give you a garden, Percy Gauss said.

But can you give me a smelly Fascist dictator with blood on his hands who comes into my bed at night and kills all my plants and then demands an apology? I did not say this.

– You are thinking of Dolores López, he then said. I have room for her too. Please say something, Francis.

– I don't quite know what to say, Percy.

– It is all rather sudden, I know. Ah, shall we order?

A waiter had appeared.

– The sole, I think, Jerome, said Percy, with mashed potatoes and a bottle of the—

He murmured the name of a certain pricey Chablis with which I was once on familiar terms.

– Same for me, I said.

– Perhaps I should leave it with you, he then said. Not a decision to be made quickly. You will have your own concerns, of course.

He lifted a hand, gestured vaguely in the direction of my own concerns.

– One question, I said.

– And what's that?

– How does Gilly feel about it?

91

– She wants you to be comfortable and secure, with us.

– But, Percy, are you sure that *you* want me comfortable and secure, with you? I come with baggage, you know.

– I am aware of that.

Oh no you're not, I thought. Not my baggage. I didn't say this either.

– You're right, I said, this is all rather sudden. May I think about it for a few days? I must say, though, this is most generous of you, Percy.

– Not at all, old man. Ah, the wine. Just pour, will you?

The meal proceeded in a civilised manner, and once or twice I reverted to the initial topic, and asked him what sort of a garden it was, and if there was a room I might have for a study, anything would do. Pantry. Attic. Woodshed. All *camouflage*, of course, all *persiflage* – I would never move out of Cleaver Square. They would have to carry me out, feet first. That house, been in my family seventy years, no, eighty. More! More to the point, it was haunted now, or I was haunted, rather, and strange though it may sound, it's not a thing one can walk away from as easily as all that. Probably bring the thing with me. This was not an idea a gent like Percy Gauss would understand. Gilly might. Perhaps that was why she had left it to him to make the overture. She knew it was futile, for she too had seen the *generalísimo*. Yes. I was sure of it now. It was there in her face, in her *skin*. What was happening to my garden, it was beginning to happen to my daughter. Her translucent skin was starting in places to crease, and to pucker. One morning I had glimpsed a distinct *splotchiness*, not unlike the discoloration I'd observed in my hydrangeas. Had Percy not seen it?

We lapsed into silence. I asked him what news from Madrid, and all that could be said now, he told me, was that Franco had not long to live, and that we could hope for better with his successor. And who might that be? I said. He murmured the name of Juan Carlos de Borbón, the crown prince.

– We've known this for some time, he then remarked as he groped about in his pocket.

– A monarchist, are you, Percy?

– Only way back to democracy, I'm afraid.

– Now, Percy, I said, let me ask you something.

Out with his little silver lighter and he tried to spark up a thin cigar.

– Francis, please.

– Do you really intend to marry Gillian?

He removed the cigar from between his lips and gave out a shout – Ha! – leaned across – laid narrow white fingers on this bony purple hand of mine, clasped it warmly, in fact, and oh, slight tremor in the loins, I'm afraid, and I thought, life in the old dog yet but I can't really be doing with it any more. There was a pleasant smell off him too, an expensive cologne, Charvet, I do think. Nobody touches you after seventy except doctors, as a rule. A sister, if you're lucky enough to have one. Undertakers.

– My dear Francis, he said – he paused, grew serious, held my eye – puffed at the cigar, a mellow aroma – as a matter of fact, he said, yes, I do intend to marry Gillian. But the point is, do you approve?

He removed his hand and sat back, watching me close. I lifted my chin, frowned, cast my own eyes down, considered clasping *his* hand but thought the better of it. I leaned forward.

– I do, I said. I do approve. I like you, Percy. But I will never live in your house.

– No, he said thoughtfully, I thought not.

There. I had told him. Now it was time for me to go. I got myself up out of my chair, and he organised a taxi, and waved me off from the front steps. I sank back in the cab, exhausted, but not altogether displeased with my performance, given all I had to deal with then. But as we swung up round Buckingham Palace – by force of habit I spat a big gob into my hanky, no friend of the monarchy, I! – I was assailed with a kind of form-less anxiety once more, which was followed by a more distinct disquiet, of which the cause was clear. It was this glimpse I'd caught of a future in which Gilly's atten-tion would shift entirely to Percy Gauss, and she'd move out of Cleaver Square, and I'd be left to die alone. Yes, alone, and quite possibly mad, or madder at least than I already was.

When I got home Gilly was in the kitchen and so was Finty. Gilly asked me if it had gone well and I said I thought we'd had a fine time.

– Oh, Pa! What did you expect?

– Darling, I had to be sure he was a gentleman.

There was hooting. Finty asked me with some facetiousness since when I'd been interested in gentlemen. Only all my life, I whispered. So I played the fool, but inside I was crying.

19

I T BECAME APPARENT within twenty-four hours, less, that Gilly had spoken to Percy and learned of my refusal to move into his house on Lord North Street. I would say there was a distinct darkening of the mood in Cleaver Square, accompanied by an almost palpable silence that hung in the corridors and common rooms of this old Georgian house like a fog, with contributions from Finty, who manifested small flashes of ill temper which rather annoyed me, my sister being technically in fact a *guest*, even if she had been born in the house, grown up in it, and maintained her own monastic cell in the attic for more years than I could remember. I retired to my study, where I was joined by Henry Threshold, who liked the atmosphere in the house no better than I did.

From time to time one or other of the women would open my door and say, tersely, 'Lunch,' or 'Drinks,' and I would bestir myself; and for two or three days the household lurched on in some kind of routine but in an atmosphere so dense with displeasure you could cut it with a bone-saw. I was in the doghouse. I was in disgrace. Fortunately I had much to preoccupy me at the time – not least, the stolen poems – also, I had something of an escape hatch. If I was quiet about it I could slip out unseen in the late morning and cross the square, and often enough I'd find Hugh Supple scribbling away in the saloon bar of the Earl of Rochester, where I'd be greeted with a good deal more warmth than I got at home.

It seemed Hugh was serious about this plan he'd spoken of a week or two earlier, of writing a long piece for the *Manchester Guardian* about my experiences in Spain as a way to provide what he called *a living context* to the poetry. Was I flattered? Of course I was. I was also aware that when he'd first come to the house, earlier in the summer, I'd told him rather angrily that I had no desire whatsoever to talk about Spain. Well, it seems I did. And perhaps he had shown himself to possess a sufficiently sympathetic ear, and a reasonable grasp of the general background of the civil war, that it was not so difficult to share with him a few of my stories. Also, he had rather a nice bottom. He had been not unaware of the tenderness with which I spoke about Doc Roscoe, and said he was curious to know what it had been like to be in Madrid with him in the early months of the war.

– Bloody nightmare, I said. You know, of course, that if you think you can demoralise a city by bombing it, even with German aircraft, you'll usually find the reverse is true. It excites people. Stiffens their sinews. The people of Madrid – their contempt for Fascist bombs was extraordinary. Such a brave people. Lot of debauchery about too, lot of – loose behaviour. Where there's fear and danger there's sex, my experience.

I may have regarded him with rather sleepy eyes, and even a faint suggestion of a leer. No. I doubt it. I am not a man who leers. Hugh then said that yes, he'd read about this. And then, surely, he said, what about the spirit of the Blitz? Defiance and courage and so on? He knew I'd been in London for most of Hitler's war, so I'd have seen all that too.

– I saw people driven mad, I said.

– I'm sure you did.

– To lose your house? Your family? To be left with nothing at all?

I'd spoken with more feeling than I'd intended. I seemed to be confronting my own personal blitz. I'd had rather a bad shock that morning myself. I'd come out of my study into the hall downstairs and found beside the front door three suitcases and a cardboard box half filled with books, although not my books, of course, Gilly's books. I'd gone into the kitchen, see what was up. There she was going through the cutlery drawer, sorting into heaps on the kitchen table our knives and forks and spoons and such.

– Oh, there you are, she'd said. There's tea in the pot.

– What are you doing, darling?

– We can't leave it all to the last minute, Pa.

– Are you taking everything?

Here she stopped what she was doing and turned to me.

– Pa, she said, you're not going to need a dozen table settings, now are you? Might as well take them with me, I can't see Dolores López polishing them once a week.

So I told Hugh Supple about this – it wasn't really his business, but I had to speak to someone – I'd get no sympathy from Finty – and what I said was that for the first time the reality of my situation had properly dawned on me. I was being *left behind*.

– What about the furniture? I'd said to Gilly.

– You'll have enough. I'll leave all the old stuff.

So there I sat, in the saloon bar of the Earl of Rochester, telling nice Hugh Supple that my house was being dismantled under my nose, and Gilly was going to leave me 'the old stuff'.

I saw his concern. Would I still be able to live there, he wanted to know.

– The old stuff, I said. She's leaving me the old stuff.

– Can I help? he said.

I gazed at him. What a dear boy he was. Could he help? My dread, my irritation, it all just drained away. I touched his cheek. I was still not sure if he shaved three times a day or never.

– Can you help? Dear boy, you're helping me quite enough as it is. Don't worry about it, I shouldn't have mentioned it. I'm not going anywhere.

Still he looked worried.

– Nor are you, I hope, I said.
– I have no plans to.
– Good boy. Where were we? The Blitz. Big orgy.
– Madrid?
– Of course.

20

W HAT I FIRST remember is running, for my life, as it felt, and that was in Madrid, and I don't remember where I was running but I think possibly the Gran Vía and I was more terrified than I have ever been in my life. And it was a function of seeing a German fighter plane rise suddenly from behind a building, extraordinary sight! – just appearing from below, from nowhere, as it seemed – and loosing off a belt of ammunition in my direction. And I took off running. And he pursued me as though it were sport, and dusk was coming on as I darted and feinted and I sprinted and I flung myself into doorways, to no avail. I had no time to be terrified, not with a Heinkel behind me, low over the broad avenue, its bullets lifting clouds of dust from mortar and brickwork and concrete, and the only idea in my head was of this malignant German intent on killing me, and if a man ever needed rescuing it was I, and I was.

– You were?

This was Hugh. He was scribbling away with his tongue between his teeth, from time to time pushing a hand through his riotously untidy hair, and whenever I paused he murmured, go on, go on.

How long it lasted I don't remember, perhaps a few seconds but it hardly mattered, but on this deserted street a man was standing in a doorway that gave onto a courtyard, and until this moment every door I'd passed had been shuttered and bolted and I'd found myself trapped as though in a blind alley, but this man pulled me through a door and into the courtyard beyond, where I stood with my head against the wall, panting, and vomiting a little in my throat.

– Hey, buddy.

I looked at Hugh.

– That's what he said, I said. Hey, buddy.

– Go on.

So I told Hugh how I got my breath back and took a look at this chap, who was wearing an International Brigade tunic. I tried to say something but he told me to can it, shut up, he was trying to listen to something. I thought it was the Heinkel coming back. I'd slumped to the ground.

– I'm sure, said Hugh.

The guy had his head up still. The city was under air attack. We heard gunshot and bombs, and sirens, and shouting from nearby. Again I started to speak—

– Listen, chum—

He knelt beside me and put his hand on my mouth, the other tight on my shoulder. He held me there, staring off, and listening intently. Then his eyes were on me. And I heard it too.

A cry. Very quiet and from not far away.

– Come with me, he whispered.

He took his hand from my mouth, leaving a smoky, chalky taste, not unpleasant. I stood up. He stepped along the inside wall of the courtyard to a door in the corner and I followed him. We were very cautious now. We pressed ourselves against the wall. It was almost dark, moonless, late twilight on a December night, and Madrid under attack from German aircraft—

Again we heard the cry. My companion – his name was Doc Roscoe, I discovered later that night – made a low, answering cry, and the voice responded. We pushed open the door in the corner of the courtyard and came upon a scene of utter devastation. The roof had collapsed, several interior walls had come down, it was thick with dust and there were fallen timbers across the floor, for the damage was so recent – a bomb, or several bombs – that the rubble had not yet settled, and there was movement, and several fires burning, but there was also that human sound, the cry that my companion had been listening for.

Then he was picking a path across heaps of unstable rubble towards a figure some yards away, ghostlike in the gloom, and trying to lift a fallen beam.

There was a woman trapped under it. We added our strength and the beam came up, showering sparks.

103

We were too late, she was dead, but then from under this dead woman all at once a small child crawled out, I will never forget it – like a little black frog emerging from under a stone! A life – literally – tousled, filthy, a small girl, alive, and we hauled her clear but I couldn't hold the beam so this Doc Roscoe took it and somehow I pulled out the mother's body, then we heard more aircraft and we fled the building with the child lifted clear, clutching my new friend round his neck. As for the ghostlike figure, he must have slipped away, we didn't see him go.

When we reached the street it was dark but no longer deserted. People were running through the shadows, bombs were still exploding and walls falling, and fires erupting, men and women fleeing past barricades built of paving stones, there was much shouting, and some screaming. We ran until we found a bridge over a canal and crawled under it. The child hadn't uttered a sound.

Now Hugh was interested in my American friend, Doc.

– Was there any – I mean, what did he—

– Do? Doc? He saved the day.

He was not scribbling now. He was listening.

– How?

What was he after, some telling moment, a word, a gesture, an unspoken current of whatever it is that the brave offer the weak in moments like this? I tried to remember, only because I wanted him to understand the sort of man Doc was.

We were sitting on the towpath, I told Hugh, and I remembered it all so clearly now, we were under a low bridge, having run through streets as bombs fell and buildings collapsed and with the little girl still safe in Doc's arms. He was examining her, and she didn't make a sound, but she kept her eye covered with her hand, so Doc gently removed it, and we saw at once that the eyelid was red and swollen and all closed up.

– You a medic?

– Ambulance.

He had me push down the child's eyelid as far as I could, then lift it. He sat with his back to the brickwork of the bridge while I knelt before the girl. I shone my torch into her eye. I had to get in very close to her face. She blinked the eye a few times, it was the left one, and Doc said I'd have to wash it out. He told me to get a piece of gauze from his pack, and a flask of drinking water.

Now Hugh Supple was scribbling away with great zeal.

My face was close to the girl's and Doc was crouched beside me, observing intently, and we were two dirty, unshaven men with a small girl between us, all clustered together under that bridge, herself bravely clutching a small cloth doll.

– Get it over, to her nose.

I was right on top of her with the torch between my teeth, and the water and the gauze ready to hand. Doc was beside me, holding up the eyelid with his little finger and telling the child to keep her head back and not blink. I still heard falling bombs but they seemed further away

105

now, as I poured a very little water into her upturned eye and some of it spilled down her cheek but she was very good, very still, and Doc held her hands, murmuring to her. Then in I gently went, with the pinched corner of the gauze, in the narrow beam of the torch, and I was able to push the tiny fragment of grit over towards her nose as Doc had told me, and then the tear glands started to flow. In a second I had the grit out and onto her cheek, just as we heard a large explosion rather too close. Then she was blinking the eye and it was all right. She shook her head a little and I was still crouched before her as the explosions got closer once more.

For a couple of seconds we didn't move. Our three faces were an inch apart. We were straining to hear. I remember the child's expression, it was utter trust. Brave little thing! Then Doc said we'd better get the hell away from that bridge, and we were on the move again, and the eye was clean now, and I was no longer afraid, and later I would remember those few moments so very clearly, and how Doc looked after both of us.

– And when you got back out on the street? said Hugh.

Then it was very strange, I told him. People huddled in doorways, shouting names into the darkness, some sitting on steps, crying, and the dust rising and already bells and sirens, and the flares where men and women searched for survivors in rubble that was still smoking and shifting, and would you believe it, I said, I saw a man run across the street to where a trembling, terrified young girl was leaning against a wall trying to light a cigarette. And you know what he did?

Hugh looked up. I looked at him, nodding.

– He put his own cigarette between the girl's lips.

– Then what happened?

– They went off together.

– Complete strangers?

– Not any more.

– And the next morning? In the daylight?

I put my glass down on the table and stared at him now with some astonishment.

– How should I know?

– No, no, he cried, touching my arm, I mean what was it like in the streets?

And so on. By the time I left the pub he was starting to get the picture, or so I hoped. And as for the little girl – it was Dolores López, of course – later I sent her to London on a refugee ship out of Valencia, through the Red Cross. I gave instructions she be taken to Cleaver Square, where my sister Finty would receive her, and I can only imagine the reception she received. Finty, herself childless, taking in this small frightened girl who'd lost her family in the bombing of Madrid, and been sent to her to be looked after – small wonder a bond was established between those two, which remains strong to this day; they were like mother and daughter from the first. Finty taught herself Spanish solely for the sake of Dolores López, who did learn English, and could speak it when she had to, but she preferred not to. Why? Who knows? *¿Quien sabe?* Perhaps it had something to do with what she suffered during the bombing of Madrid. We didn't force her.

Later Doc and I sat smoking in the back of my ambulance, parked down an alley, with our legs hanging out. Dolores López was still with us then, fast asleep on one of the stretchers, clutching her little cloth doll. Doc asked me what had brought me to Spain.

– Boredom, I said.

Not entirely candid but he was amused. Nobody wants to take the high ground, spout on about stopping the march of fascism. Doc was as tall as I but he had more sinew to him, and his hair was cropped and bristled the American way. He had dusty boots and a tunic like any International Brigade soldier in Madrid then. He asked me drily if it wouldn't be boring to be killed.

– I think I wouldn't know.

– How difficult is it anyway? he said after a while.

– What?

– Driving this thing.

– Anyone could do it.

Everyone called him Doc, he told me. Doc Roscoe. I'll write a poem about you, I thought, and I did. More than one. Hugh said it was those poems that had first aroused his interest in what I'd seen in Spain.

We slept in the ambulance that night. It was a starry night. Too late for more bombers but the city was far from silent. In the alley where I'd left the ambulance, from a lit room somewhere above us came Spanish voices. I lit a cigarette and coughed and the voices fell silent. I remember armed men in groups, and a glimpse, once, of something I have never forgotten. Four men in the early morning forcibly escorting a fifth man, terrified, in bare feet, crying out, struggling, down the street and round a corner, all of which we watched, Doc and I, in the certainty that this flailing barefoot man was about to be stood against a wall and shot. Soon enough we heard the shot. Fifth column. There were spies everywhere. This was Madrid in late 1936. And while the Fascists' grip elsewhere in the country was only tightening, Madrid held out.

And as for Doc, three days later I was working beside him in a front-line aid post near the university. And there the fighting was really very fierce indeed.

I let myself in through the front door and found that the suitcases in the hall had gone but there was another box of books. A third cardboard box was on the kitchen table, half filled with plates and bowls wrapped in tissue paper. It was frankly deeply unsettling, all this sudden evidence of *transience*; and McNulty, thereby, abandoned.

I went into my study and closed the door behind me. I'd only had a bag of crisps for lunch. I thought I might find Henry Threshold on the rug or in the armchair but he was nowhere to be seen. Talking about Doc did make me maudlin. But it was a mercy, I supposed, that the changing season, and the imminent coming of winter, of darkness, I mean, and cold, would conceal from these old eyes the damage done to the garden I had nurtured for so many years, although perhaps I'd seen the best of it, I thought, or the last of it. Ha.

Feeling slightly ill I turned away from the window. I settled myself in the armchair. Gratefully I permitted the soporific function of several small sherries to take effect, and closed my eyes.

> *To die, to sleep;*
> *To sleep, perchance to dream:*
> *Ay, there's the rub:*
> *For in that sleep of death what dreams may come—*

I awoke with a start! I damn near fell out of the armchair!

The door was flung open. Gilly rushed in.

– Pa! What happened? Have you had a nightmare?

Did I have a nightmare? Oh, I had a nightmare all right. Oh, God save me from these bloody nightmares. Frankly I don't know how many more of them I can take.

21

GONE, THE CHILLY hauteur of my offended daughter, who packed her books in cardboard boxes and told me she'd leave me 'the old stuff'. Now she was at my side with her fingers on my chill damp brow, and behind her in the doorway stood Dolores López.

– Oh God, Gilly, I said, and began to cry.

She got me organised in the armchair and asked me if I might not be happier upstairs in bed but no, I wanted to stay downstairs, safer here, people around, and Henry was over by the fireplace now, watching these events with intense concentration. Soon there came a hot cup of tea with a splash of brandy in it, and Dolores López even attempted to spread a blanket on my knees, but I was having none of that, no blankets, Dolores, I cried – *¡no quiero una manta!* – too redolent altogether of the bath chair and the old party mumbling and dribbling as he readied himself for the final curtain. No, a hot spiked cup of tea and Henry Threshold, that was all I needed, and of course evidence that in spite of everything my daughter still loved me and would come to me if she heard me in distress.

In distress. Oh yes. I'd been in distress all right. I was with Doc and we were in freezing turbulent waters and I was struggling to stay afloat, and Doc was trying to help me but he couldn't hold on to me because I kept slipping from his grasp, and he kept going under because I was pulling him under with me, trying to get my arms round his neck because I was panicking, and we were both going to drown—

I must have woken up then, with the cry that brought Gilly and Dolores López to my study, and you may imagine the state I was in as I lurched into wakefulness in the armchair. Gilly of course wanted to know what I'd been dreaming about but this one I could never speak of. I'd told her the one about the *garrote* but this was altogether far too, I don't know, far too—

– Pa, you look very pale. I think I might call Dr Gent.

– No, you won't. I'm fine, Gilly. Just one of my dreams.

– I think this was a very bad one. You screamed.

– Oh, I don't think I screamed. *Dolores, ¿grité yo?*

– *Sí, Señor Francis, chilliste como una muchachita. Tuviste mucho miedo en le voz.*

– *¿Como una muchachita? ¿De veras?*

Screaming like a little girl – hardly surprising, a dream like that. And poor Doc! But why ever would I want to pull Doc into freezing water with me? I loved that man. I never meant to do him harm—

Oh Christ. Now I felt as though I'd killed him all over again.

– Gilly, I'm all right, I said.

But I was very far from all right. It would take me some time to sink this one back into the primal slime. Did I have a nightmare?

Yes, dear.

22

S o I was, yes, a bit shaky when next I crossed Cleaver
Square to see Hugh Supple in the Earl of Rochester.
It seemed absurd to tell him I could no longer talk
about Spain, that the cost was too prohibitive, that my
teetering psyche wasn't up to it, couldn't handle it any
longer – what would he think? But did it matter what
he thought? Well, oddly – and as I write this I am in
my study on a grey Sunday afternoon – oddly, no it
didn't. He is a charming young man, of course, but
for all his reading, and all his astute probing, there are
certain aspects of Spain that have escaped his notice.
He takes the Spaniard to be a sort of Englishman but
with a rather more colourful political history. This is
not the case. They were fanatical, the young *milicianos*,
as I knew them, I mean the sort of boys who joined a
Republican militia. They ran on heat, flame and steam,
I tell Hugh, that's what was in them, I say. And I saw

violent tendencies in those young men of the militias, I say, violent tendencies, yes, and wild courage, and reckless commitment, for they loved their young republic, but the point was that their republic was in mortal danger from men determined to destroy it. And these men, these Fascists, had the support of the Church, and the landowners, and the middle class and the aristocracy—

When I spoke to Hugh about this I saw his pale blue eyes grow wet and bright at the thought of what those militia boys had had to face. He asked me for the telling incident, but telling incidents escape me now, except for those that are burnt not into my mind, no, but into my soul.

I talked about the Battle of the Jarama, and how we heard the bells from the monastery at Santa Inez ringing out across the valley as we settled at night in shallow trenches with a little straw thrown down, up on the ridge, and then there was silence but for an occasional rifle shot, or an aircraft passing over. So there we were up above the valley, among the olive groves, with the moonlit Jarama sweeping in great shining curves across the plain below, and with far too much open ground for our liking. You saw the land rise on the far side of the valley, and in the distance to the north lay Madrid, almost invisible now, as very few lights burned at night.

It was February 1937, I said. Winter. Doc had set up an aid post in an old farmhouse. The Moors overran us. We were taken in the back of an open lorry to a monastery in the village of Santa Eulalia, and locked in cells once used by monks.

– And what happened?

But I was exhausted.

– Enough, dear boy. Tomorrow.

I have not spoken about the Jarama in years. The old fellows in the Bull mention it from time to time. They know I was there. But there's an understanding among us that each is entitled to his silence, should he prefer not to speak of those days. I'm not alone in my reluctance. Anyway I was transferred to Málaga soon after. Nobody wants to intrude on another man's secrets. The reason I survived when others died is my business. War is rarely tidy, never clean. We all know that.

23

So I say to Hugh, yes, it is the telling incident that escapes me now. But at the same time I can't deny that I have a story, and now someone who wants to hear it. If I could only bring myself to tell him. Poor Hugh. He has an old boy on his hands who cannot reveal the one story that matters, and for the simple reason that he is too ashamed to tell it. So he and I sit in silence in the late-morning stillness in the Earl of Rochester, this last autumn, as I have come to think of it, and I have Johnny make me a gin and tonic rather weaker than the one he'd given me the morning I'd fled across the square from Mrs Doris Withers, and I continue to cling to that which I have sworn to myself I will never divulge to a living soul.

On occasion I have him over to the house, which is somewhat depleted by Gilly now, although my study is comfortable enough, if overwhelmed rather by books and papers and such. He reminds me one morning that when we first met, that rainy day he'd come to Cleaver Square with the photographer, I'd said: *I see him still.* So I tell him about the appearance of the *generalísimo* in the garden, how he'd stood there in my hydrangeas, and of the faint distinct tang of the morgue he carried on him, and the uncertain purpose of his presence. I avoid talking about his more intimate visits to my bedroom, and my bed, if it had in fact been him in my bed, because it might have been my father, or his ghost, rather – I don't know. I don't want to find out.

– So the general, he says, is a night visitor also?

– On occasion, I say.

– But an apparition.

Moment of truth, you might think. Silence.

– Will you tell me more about him?

He was in the armchair under my reading light, avid and curious in an untidy grey suit with argyle socks and old black oxfords, his thin legs crossed and the notebook in his lap. The yellow pencil was as ever in his fingers, and his eyes were bright. I was at my desk with the chair swivelled round into the room. Throw him a bone, I thought.

– He is always in uniform, I said.

– Can you describe the uniform?

I'd been through this with Gillian. Stained green serge, I told him, blue sash, red tassels, riding boots, cap.

– Wait!

I went into one of my desk drawers and pulled out the paper bag with the torn patch of green serge in it

118

which I'd found in the hydrangeas. It stank. It was really rather disgusting. Hugh didn't want to touch it.

– No medals?

So I talked about the foliated Spanish eagle in gold, and the arm-of-service insignia, crossed muskets under a double bugle. I even mentioned the red diamond on each collar point.

– Cap?

– Six-pointed stars.

– Clean?

– Hardly. Smells like a morgue.

– Could you tell me what he says to you?

– I could.

Silence.

– But you would prefer not to.

More silence. I would prefer not to. I was suddenly irritated with him. In his hunger for the vivid detail, the telling incident, I felt I was being pumped. I know this about newspapermen, having been one myself, once, for a while; what they really want is to drink your blood.

– But you do converse with him?

– I listen to him.

– Will you tell me what he says?

– He weeps.

Hugh Supple rocked back very slightly in the armchair and dropped his pencil. Some frowning now, a knitting of the brows.

– For what? he then said, sitting forward a little, as he groped down the side of the armchair for his pencil,

119

and apparently choosing his words with some care. For what does General Franco weep?

– For whom, you mean.

Ask not for whom the ghoul weeps, I thought. I was beginning to enjoy myself. I liked his little recoil. He waited for me to elaborate. A tricky inquisitor, this one, but I was not to be had so easily. I may have been haunted, you see, but I wished to be haunted on my own terms.

– Yes, for whom.

– Luis Carrero Blanco.

He knew who Carrero Blanco was. That man's immortal soul was black as pitch – straight to hell for that one! I was about to enlarge on the theme but Hugh glanced at his watch and said he was very sorry but he had to go. Could we resume next week, he said, if I didn't mind? – as he extricated himself from the quagmire-like depths of my armchair.

24

B UT HE IS such a good boy. It's true I become irritated with him at times but he is never so gauche as to challenge me on the large epistemological question, by which I mean he never appears to doubt my accounts of the sightings or asks me how the *generalísimo* can be in Madrid and London at the same time. Suffice to say it is a source of great pleasure to spend an hour in that quiet saloon bar, misty autumn sunlight slanting through the top of the window, complete with dancing motes, or in my study, better still, with this articulate and very attractive young man who can talk about, oh, Swinburne, and world religions, and the origins of Roman law as it pertains to the Spanish Inquisition, and who writes for the *Manchester Guardian*, and who sometimes scribbles away while I tell him of my experiences in the civil war in Spain, and how I am haunted by the *generalísimo*.

And had I ever met him in the flesh?

– Once, I said.

This was not strictly true but I was in jaunty temper.

– And?

We were in the pub that morning. I didn't want to tell him yet about that certain Spanish captain, whose leg Doc and I had amputated. I gazed at him wordlessly, my expression one of, oh, reluctant discretion. Tactful reticence. I may have produced a quiet sigh. I may have murmured, *dear boy*. There were moments when the sunlight seemed to catch fire in his shaggy hair – Hugh's, I mean – which gleamed then like damp sand at sunset with the tide going out. Then I'd notice the clock over the counter and – *Time I was getting home*, I might cry, for I don't wish to be rude.

I cross Cleaver Square with its scattering of dead and dying leaves, and for once with a good brisk spring in my step.

25

THAT BRISK STEP was of course due to the presence in my life of this new friend, young Hugh, for whom I nursed a quiet, largely unspoken affection, while all too aware that this was likely the last experience I would have of tender companionship such as he offered: I am old. I am old! Shout it from the rooftops: he is old! Whether Hugh understood this I rather doubt. He wanted my story and found me not too tedious a companion, I hope. I don't think he suspected that my feelings for him were in any way untoward, or perhaps he did, and didn't mind. Oh, but I am a grotesque! Surely—

It hardly matters now.

I was at this time relieved to have had no further sightings, not since the day I was with Mrs Doris Withers in the sitting room, when I'd again glimpsed him in the hydrangeas – *him*, I say – *it*, rather, glimpsed *it*, for I had begun to see *it* for what it was, and what it was was not a man, nor even a ghost. Gilly seems pleased that I am now comporting myself as a dignified semi-demented old gent ought to, although I think she has no very great confidence that this new friendship of mine will work out at all well; they seldom do.

Meanwhile she continues filling boxes with books and pans and bedding and such, and says no more about my decision to stay behind in Cleaver Square. I know she wants me to live with herself and Percy in Lord North Street, but she isn't harassing me, in fact she never speaks of it at all now. We are getting along rather well, she and I.

Finty, a different story. I am very displeased with her. How could she imply, as she did when I first protested the presence of Mrs Withers in the house, that I had been consulted, and had agreed, but had forgotten all about it? I ask you: is that likely? If so, then she might say anything she wanted, and when I contradicted her, or otherwise resisted an assault on my much-vaunted cognitive acumen, she could reply – *Francis, we discussed this and you agreed.* And I would say – *Oh, I don't remember that!* And she would say – *Exactly! Precisely! That's just the problem!*

26

MEANWHILE I HAVE not ceased my investigations into the nature and history of my so-called apparition. I visited the London Library. There I came upon the work of a scholar at the University of Cairo, a learned woman who has made a study of pre-Islamic ghouls. She found one in Mesopotamia called *gallu*, and claims it for a descendant of the North African desert ghoul. It too is a resident of the wilderness, but entirely dissimilar from others of its kind, including the *si'lwah*, which apparently haunts lavatories and other waste areas and is a source of considerable interest in itself.

One story she quotes involves a Muslim caliph who encountered a female ghoul in the desert. This ghoul turned its head completely round in an attempt to frighten him, so he cut off its head with his sword. I had briefly entertained a similar solution to my own problem, I mean the *generalísimo*, but frankly doubted I was capable of decapitating anything more dangerous than a dead flower. Later scholars, I learn, argue that ghouls do not exist but are in fact quasi-spectral cultural expressions of contemporary social anxieties. That may be, but the fact is that belief in the ghoul, particularly among the Berber tribes, has never died, and for good reason in my opinion: for they are still around. I have one in my garden.

Hugh Supple eagerly listens to my accounts of life in the medieval monastery at Santa Eulalia, where I was imprisoned with Doc Roscoe and a number of Englishmen and several of the young *milicianos* who had reinforced the British Battalion on Suicide Hill, as we came to call that fatal ridge above the Jarama. Hugh was curious about an offhand remark I'd made about the monastery, that *death stalked the place*. I tell him there was a period when over the course of four nights forty-three men were shot there. And we were certain, Doc and I, that our turn was soon to come. He was stoic, phlegmatic, just as I would have expected. And as you might also expect, he watched me closely, alert for signs of distress. He was by far the strongest of us.

As for the priest, we would hear him whispering to the young men in the cells on our cloister at dead of night, before they made their way out to the courtyard, under guard, and with the Angelus bell tolling from the tower nearby. He would be telling them that they need not be afraid, for death was to be welcomed, for it brought release.

126

– Could *you* say that, I ask Hugh Supple, to a boy about to face a firing squad?

He took the question seriously. He of course had no inkling of what it was like to be under sentence of death. A discrepancy arises in the mind of the condemned man, I told him. Of course he *knows* he is going to die, but at the same time he does not *believe* it. We were in my study that day, himself in the armchair, I at my desk. The weather was colder now, and I needed the electric fire. I have to admit I had grown dependent on this young man's company, for the simple reason that I was experiencing intimations of my own mortality, in particular during nights of bad dreams and wakeful anxiety. I know I am going to die, and now I am starting to believe it.

– No, said Hugh, I could not say that.

– Why not? It might give comfort.

– Because the word *release* suggests they were constrained before.

– So they were.

– So you execute a man to release him from the constraints you have imposed on him yourself?

I tell him I will have to think about that.

Often my dreams seem no more than variations of memories of the time I spent in the monastery, and which I arouse now so as to keep Hugh entertained. Nights were the worst, I told him. Despite the cold we would eventually sleep, but the hours of darkness were fractured by noises from the cloister and the courtyard beyond, and I was not alone. There were four others in the cell, Doc, of course, and three young *milicianos*, not one of them more than twenty. There was no real rest for any of us. We lay there in the bitter cold, often in silence, every one of us praying they wouldn't come for us tonight. But we'd hear them. They'd stop at a door. Then a heavy key turned in a lock. We heard the murmur of the priest. Then the shuffling boots as silent men and boys passed our door. Night after night they shuffled down the cloister past our door. And once past – we would breathe again.

The boys invented a chant. It started: *El muerto al pozo* – the dead down the hole – *el vivo al gozo* – and pleasure to the living.

El muerto al pozo, el vivo al gozo, el muerto al pozo, el vivo al gozo—

Quietly we'd chant it over and over, but soon we'd have to stop, for we were laughing like fools. Then they would talk about their families and their sweethearts, and make private jokes hard for Doc and me to follow, our Spanish was so clumsy. Ah, but there was one more trial to be borne before such silliness could begin, I told Hugh.

– What?

– After the condemned men had trudged past our door, I said, from the courtyard there would come a shout – then an order – then a volley of shots.

– Christ.

– Then silence once more. Then men's voices. But a new smell came, cordite. It drifted like string through the high Gothic window of the cell, and the Spanish boys hated it. They called it the stink of death, *olor de muerte*. They said it was sometimes smelled on bullfighters, and when it was, the man was sure to die.

Later we'd hear the rumble of lorries coming for the dead. They'd drive off into the night to distant *barrancos* where the bodies were dumped in unmarked pits and left to rot unmourned.

27

I GAZED HELPLESSLY at Hugh. I hadn't really meant to
tell him all this. Why then did I? Pride, you say: I
don't think so. Little to be proud of in this story, the
reverse. A requiem might be more apt. A Mass said for
the repose of the souls of the dead, with dirges and
solemn chants. *Requiescant in pace.* I do certainly bloody
hope so. Am I to tell you of all the great things Doc did?

– The great things? said Hugh.

You catch his tone, yes? The merest hint, almost imper-
ceptible, but present nonetheless, undeniably so, of the
sceptic's hesitation – the hand on the wall, for balance,
the foot lifted, the step not taken—

– Great things?

Two men sit at a small round table in an empty pub
in south London, one young, one old. One strong, one
frail. Faint concentric rings on the table, imprints of
a thousand beer glasses. Cigarette burns too. Hugh is

cautious. He no longer scribbles in his little three-ringed notebook quite as assiduously as once he did. It has occurred to me that he no longer believes me. Or if he believes, what he believes is no longer the dogma of the one true church of St Doc, so – take him away! Bring in the Jesuits – *and let the torture begin!*

But we live in more enlightened times, ha. Young Hugh Supple is to be permitted his doubts and scruples. Shall I remind him of a tenement building in the slums of Madrid that was hit by explosives and incendiaries, and how we plunged into thick smoke, Doc and I, with rags tied round our faces, because Doc had heard a child's cry? And of how he had me lift a charred beam, ash and embers raining down upon me while he retrieved from beneath that beam a screaming child—

– It was Dolores López, said Hugh rather wearily.

It was indeed! Only survivor of the fire in which her entire family perished that night. Then to be swept up into the arms of the American doctor, and carried to safety through all the confusion and destruction of that hellish night – had I already told him the story, and if so, why not, what else was I to do with it? I may also have told Hugh how he amputated the Spanish captain's leg on a table in the back of my ambulance, behind the front line on Suicide Hill, and nobody could have saved that man's life but he did, and the captain survived, a *falangista*, yes, but that mattered little to Doc whether the poor wretch on the table was a Republican or what he was, and with my help, and some iodine, a bottle of transfused blood, a little morphine and a thorough debridement of the wound, with a splash of Dakin's solution in it – all this to forestall a fulminating infection, with tetanus and gas gangrene the inevitable concomitants – and a good sharp bone-saw – as we heard a machine gun briefly rattle, an incoherent shouting in the darkness. Under a single bulb, with a torch in his hand, Doc peered into the wound he'd already opened with a scalpel, and started to discard damaged tissue into a bucket at his feet—

At last he stepped back and asked for the saw.

On a stretcher on the floor lay another man, this one with a chest wound, groaning. Others were waiting outside, on other bloodied stretchers.

In the flickering gloom I handed him the bone-saw.

Hugh is nodding but he isn't scribbling. I fall silent. He may have heard it all before, I frankly don't remember, but with each telling new details come to mind, and the picture becomes more complete, and is this not the point, to elucidate the truth? I say this.

A silence.

Not all silences are the same. You will have noticed this yourself, reader. I shall call this one portentous. It contained multitudes. It *portended*. But what did it portend? In Cleaver Square someone was whistling. Somewhere a car horn sounded. All this I heard during that silence. Hugh wouldn't meet my eye.

– Do you think I'm inventing this? I said, as I set my glass down on the table. He cut the man's leg off. Up here!

132

I showed him the place. It was high on my thigh, not far from the groin.

– I think you exaggerate.

Another silence, this one of a different quality. Clearly he's been talking to Gilly.

– Hugh, may I ask you something?

– Of course.

I'd got him on the left foot now. He hadn't expected me to be calm.

– Have you read Schopenhauer?

– Should I have?

– Perhaps.

– Why?

– He may have something to teach you about a godless cosmos in which man flourishes only by means of knowledge and contemplation and compassion.

– You think I lack compassion?

The night they came for us – when it was our turn to go along the cloister with the priest, with the Angelus bell chiming in the canons' tower – something happened that I hadn't yet told him about. It occurred to me now that I never would.

He was flipping through his notebook, glancing up once or twice, searching presumably for what notes he might have taken about an amputation.

– But this man was your enemy, he said.

It was true. We'd found him unconscious on Suicide Hill and brought him in anyway.

– Doc's enemy was gas gangrene.

133

Oh, I could see Doc clearly now. It was some days later, after we'd been taken prisoner. We were in the monastery, our first night there, and it was bitterly cold. An icy fog had drifted in and our clothes were damp, and of course we had no blankets, we had nothing but what we stood up in.

Here I paused. I got up out of my chair and turned to the window to look out across Cleaver Square. It was empty. Oh, where, *where* was Henry? It was two days already, more, and no sight of him. I sat down again. I resumed. Then Doc woke up, I said.

– What? Wait! Where are we?

– In the monastery. In our cell. He got to his feet and stretched himself like a cat.

I watched the reaction of my young friend. A shake of the head, at least, at the idea of Doc Roscoe waking up refreshed in that place. But he was feeling the cold now, I said, he was clapping his hands and blowing out air like smoke, and then he looked at this sorry group, three shivering Spanish boys, with one poncho between them, and myself, and all rubbing ourselves for warmth. So Doc picked his way across the flagstone floor to the door – and here I stood up in the empty saloon bar of the Earl of Rochester, and pretended to be Doc Roscoe, hands spread wide like a tightrope walker as he stepped among us. Then he started hammering on the door and shouting for the guard.

I sat down again, slowly, hands on my knees so as to keep everything in place. Johnny was leaning on the counter, reading the paper, oblivious. But I certainly had

Hugh's attention now. Well, I said. A guard eventually came and pushed open the slat in the door because Doc had been hammering on it for five minutes. In peered a bloated, unshaven face, framed in the slat in the door and stinking of wine. Doc at once demanded blankets and hot tea for these men, for whom he was the official doctor in charge. *Médico oficial a cargo*, he shouted, and the guard shouted back, saying there was no doctor here.

I had joined him at the slat in the door, and I too was shouting, *médico oficial a cargo*—

– *¡Yo el médico! ¡Yo!* shouted Doc, slapping his chest. *¡Mantas! ¡Agua! ¡Té caliente!*

I imitated him as best I could. The guard must have thought I was the doctor, I said, oh, and upon this error hinges much. Hugh had the grace to nod, at least, as though he understood. Blankets, water and hot tea, that's what Doc was demanding, and it sounded eminently reasonable to the Spanish boys, and they too gathered at the door and took up the cry, and soon from every cell along that cloister, fists and boots banging on the doors in a heavy, stamping rhythm, English and Spanish voices, chanting: *¡Mantas! ¡Agua! ¡Té caliente! ¡Mantas! ¡Agua! ¡Té caliente! Mantas*—

– I can hear it now, I said.

– Go on. What happened?

I was suddenly exhausted.

– It was no good. We knew it was no good. Why give a man hot tea and a blanket if you're going to shoot him in the morning?

135

28

WHERE WAS I? I must have dropped off.

Live thou and take thy fill of days and die
When thy day comes; and make not much of death
Lest ere thy day thou reap an evil thing.

Yes, reap an evil thing. I lived, he died. Swinburne. The poet's poet. Hugh Supple knows his work. We are in my study today. Little though I relish it I must go on, for I am embarked upon the task of giving him what I remember while I still have the wit to do so; and why it matters I am not altogether clear. But I will be derelict if I fail, and I must have murmured a few words to this effect. Hugh was frowning.

– What is it? I said.

– I don't understand what a man's leg being amputated has to do with any of this.

I will have to start again, I realise. It is important. We are in Santa Eulalia, I remind him, a medieval monastery south-east of Madrid. We are prisoners of war and we have all been sentenced to death.

– Who by?

– A military tribunal, so called. Three officers of the Falange. Hearing lasted about ninety seconds.

He nods; the notebook is out, also the yellow pencil. I tell him we are in reasonable spirits despite being very cold and under sentence of death. He is still nodding. I go on. Early one morning, I tell him, the cell door is unlocked and flung open by a guard, who steps back and there stands a Spanish officer, a colonel, bareheaded, in a thick brown overcoat open over a black uniform with belt and bandolier, and high black leather boots. This *coronel* was one of the three *falangista* officers who'd sat on that mockery of a tribunal, I tell Hugh, and sentenced us all to death.

He scribbles on.

Now the officer points at Doc Roscoe, and then at me. He turns to the guard and flicks his head up and to the side, his meaning unclear. Then he leaves.

I sit back and close my eyes. Steady, old one, I think. Don't excite yourself now. Hugh regards me, nodding, engaged.

– One question. If Doc Roscoe amputated an officer's leg, why is that officer not a prisoner himself? Of yours, I mean.

– Prisoner exchange. He's valuable to them.

– And now he's told everyone the American doctor saved his life.

137

– That is so. Can we get on?

Frowning, he scribbles. It is a very long time since last I told this story. The point is, I tell Hugh Supple, my scribbler – my *scrivener!* – that the young *capitán* who lost his leg belonged to a well-born family from Asturias, with connections to the family of María del Carmen Polo y Martínez Valdés.

– Go on, he murmurs.

– You understand, I say, who María del Carmen Polo y—

– General Franco's wife.

– That's right. And Doña María has been told that her cousin, the young *capitán*, whom apparently she favours, has suffered a terrible injury in battle; however, his life has been saved by an American doctor working for the Republicans, who is now a prisoner and sentenced to death.

I then explain to Hugh that María del Carmen Polo is the worst of women, a greedy, acquisitive creature with a passion for antiques and jewellery, which she acquires with little concern for the expense, in fact she rarely pays for what she acquires, and it is said that merchants in luxury goods stores will close up shop when she's in town.

– Nevertheless—

– Nevertheless she has a soft spot for the handsome young captain and wishes that the surgeon's life be spared.

A silence now but a different kind of silence from the earlier silence, although this one does also *portend*. I was unwilling to tell Hugh precisely what it portended because it is my shame, my henge of shame. But he has guessed it.

29

ONE NIGHT, SOMETIME after midnight, the guards unlocked our door, as we knew one night they must. We went off quietly to the courtyard. The priest came with us, murmuring useless prayers to an absent God who had forsaken all His children in Spain, as from the canons' tower came the familiar *clang! clang! clang!* of the Angelus bell; and a hand fell upon my shoulder.

But here is the horror of the thing. In those few seconds, between the hand falling on my shoulder, and the volley of gunshots, I understood what had happened. I realised their mistake. Doc Roscoe was the one they intended to spare. Not me. As we moved away from each other, he to the wall and I back to the cloister, he turned, as did I, and our eyes met. And in those few seconds I knew that we both understood perfectly what was happening to us. And that my silence was his death.

I hated him for years on account of my silence that night.

30

THE TREES IN Cleaver Square are shedding their leaves and I stand there astonished and mortified as down they drift in every hue of brown and russet and yellow. How they do crunch underfoot! And as the air grows mellow and misty, out comes the Keats, and it won't surprise you to hear that I turned my hand to an ode. I will not write it for you here, for it's no good. I have lost my muse.

But where was I? I will tell you. I have received an invitation in the post. To a wedding. To whose wedding? That of my only daughter, Gillian. To the Rt Hon. Sir Percy Gauss, MP. At Westminster Cathedral, on Victoria Street, with a reception later at the home of the happy couple in Lord North Street. But what to wear?

What to wear – as if it matters what *I* wear! A formal suit will be adequate and I do own one. I will have it cleaned. I should rather like Hugh Supple to accompany me – I think I may insist upon it. He is my only friend now, and I say this without rancour, or pathos, or any desire to arouse sympathy in my reader, if such there be, a reader, I mean, for even that I begin to doubt, as I have little enough to show for the long life I have led, and have already listed what there is to list. My two wives, both dead now. My daughter, who is about to abandon me. A dilapidated house in Cleaver Square. A few slim books of Romantic verse, all published by Hyperbole and all out of print now. The shameful tragic death of the one man I ever truly loved.

And whatever it is one *has* accomplished – how can any of it stand, given the failures that loom like great henges over a life as inconsequential as mine? *Henge*: an overhanging Neolithic stone. And here I will confess my most bitter, shaming, internally corrosive *henge*: you will have guessed it already. Doc Roscoe. When that man died I wasn't beside him and it was a mistake. I mean his death was, a mistake not merely in the grand scheme of things but in light of a careless error of which I was the unwitting beneficiary.

It was one in the morning. It had come at last. We were determined to die well. For the Spanish boys this was hardest. None of us wanted the priest. We trudged along the cloister in silence. It happened as we reached the courtyard. We shuffled in, barely a whimper from those brave frightened boys, and I saw under the flood-lights the bloody smears on the dirty, bullet-pocked wall ahead. As I stepped forward a hand fell upon my shoulder. Somebody said the word *americano*, and I was led back to the cell. But not before I heard the shouting; and then a volley of shots.

– ¡Arriba la República—!
Blam blam blam.

This now is the hard part. This is where I stand before you, or perhaps you see me on one knee – as if that were possible – my hands spread wide in supplication, for I require your benediction. I require you to accept my confession and absolve me. I could say that I did not properly learn the nature of the error until some months later, when I was transferred from the monastery to the jail in Málaga. But of course I'd guessed the truth long before that. I knew it when Doc looked at me as I was being led out of the courtyard. He knew I knew it. During the months I spent in a cell in Málaga I could think of nothing else. Later I had it confirmed that a mistake was made, and the wrong prisoner was shot. The order had come from the *generalísimo* himself.

Eventually I was shipped out and by way of Barcelona I got back to England. For years the thought was never far from me, that it should have been Doc who went home. I never attempted to find his grave. I never returned to Spain to make enquiries as to the whereabouts of those who had been shot in the monastery of Santa Eulalia. And even if I had, how would I tell his bones from another's? I could not have done so. But did that even matter? Would not one skull be as good as another? One man's ribcage, caked with soil, to serve as well as his, and

143

being exhumed, and cleaned, and coffined, and a patch of holy ground found in which to be reinterred – given at least the small uncertain solace of a decent burial under the weeping gaze of a loyal friend? Or rather: a disloyal friend. Thus do I torment myself. Thus do I measure myself, that I did not save him. He would have done it for me. He did.

And now it is too late. It has been too late for years. In the Spanish earth, in some jumble of skulls and old teeth, splintered shin bones and yellowed ribs, lie the remains of the man. I did attempt to find the family who lost a son and a brother in that foreign war, soon itself to be lost in the shadow of a greater war for which it served as mere prelude. I sent a letter to what I believed to be the family's address in New York City. I never received a reply.

Enough. The man is dead. He is long gone now, and soon I shall follow him into that bourne from which, from which – no traveller, no traveller—

Needle stuck again.

31

H<small>ENRY HAS BEEN</small> missing for four days.

32

Now Hugh tells me he wants me to speak about my childhood! I say, dear boy, you must be joking. I say, dear boy, my race is almost run, what earthly difference would it make to anything? Ask me about death and dying, that would help.

It was some days after I'd told him how Doc Roscoe, having saved the life of the Spanish *capitán*, was himself executed by firing squad. And I had other things to worry about. Henry, of course. There was the batch of poems that had gone astray. I could not think who might have gone into my desk, or why. Gilly has no interest at all in my poetry, and Finty was spending a few days in Paris with a friend. She had been rather guarded about this friend. I had no idea who he or she might be. And this is not to mention the fact that Gilly was moving out, and the house was piled high with cardboard boxes and suitcases and such. It was most unsettling.

– I'm interested in this figure you see in the garden that nobody else does, said Hugh Supple.

So he doesn't want to hear any more about Doc.

We were in my study again, still no Henry, and I was beginning to fear the worst. I thought I'd have some leaflets printed up and nail them to the trees in Cleaver Square. Someone will have seen him.

– Ghoul, I say.

I do not tell him that Dolores López sees it too.

– I suspect, may I say this, that its roots could be deeper than you think?

I gazed at him steadily, my young friend, my young Freud. My young *fraud*. Yes. I felt both flattered and irritated. I had for some years declared that I was in the postscript period of my life, my muse having departed. Put another way, the last act was just about over and the curtain was falling, and it is at this juncture that the leading man steps onto the stage, perhaps to declare an end to the proceedings and deliver a coda. Or an apologia. This is my apologia. Yes. It is not an apology, but a written defence of my opinions and conduct. Even those that are indefensible, ha.

This is my defence of the indefensible.

– You think this is all about my father.

– I think it is.

– Oh for God's sake.

I used to wonder if I would live long enough to become a ruin. There are women in Ireland, I'm told, who think about their houses in this way. Now I think I have. Become a ruin. And flattered though I may be, pleasantly astonished, even, by Hugh Supple's insatiable and all-devouring curiosity about my life, I wasn't born yesterday. And what about my mother? That saint? She ran off with Roger Dixon and who wouldn't, who could blame her, given what she suffered at the hands of poor Donald McNulty, my sad, lost, dipsomaniacal father, who could, they say, have been a great heart man.

– Francis, said Hugh, if you don't mind me saying so—

When you hear that, my experience, it means you *will* mind them saying so.

– Go on then, I said, if you must.

– You seem to have something of a persecution complex, is that fair to say?

I thought: oh, you silly boy. It was clear where he was going with this. He thought the *generalísimo* was my father. I said this.

– Yes, he said. In a manner of speaking.

– What manner is that, Doctor?

He bowed his head slightly, an adorable shy little grin briefly touching his faithless lips. I was standing with my hands on the back of my desk chair now, leaning forward towards him where he sat in the armchair under the reading lamp. I was aware I had saliva on my chin. I couldn't remember when it was that I had risen to my feet and somehow got the desk chair between myself and himself as a kind of rampart or breastwork. Flattered I may have been but there was not a chance in hell I was going to start talking about my father. It had been raining all morning and showed no sign of letting up,

148

but Henry would have found somewhere dry. Unless he lay dead in a gutter, oh God forbid—

– Your father was a doctor.

I had gone to the far end of the study where Henry often slept on the rug in front of the electric fire. With some difficulty I got down on my hands and knees. I smelled the rug. I discovered a little ball of white fur. I touched it to my cheek then put it in my pocket. I said nothing. Hugh said nothing. A minute passed. Then he spoke again.

– But you express such ambivalence towards the *generalísimo*.

– Ghoul, I murmured.

It came from where I stroked him under his chin, where he liked it.

– I beg your pardon?

– *Ghoul!* I shouted.

– Yes, of course. And your father?

– *Cardiologist!*

Another minute passed. Two. I heard Hugh rising from the armchair. I may by then have been curled up in the foetal position. Of course I wasn't.

He left. I went into the kitchen and stood at the window and looked at the garden, which was bleak and dripping in the steady downpour in this late October of the year. All at once I felt very, very sad.

Sometime later Gilly came into the kitchen. She stood beside me and together we gazed out at the garden and the rain.

– Pa, it's looking awfully dead.

149

– I know, I said.

Another sorrowful moment passed. Then I rallied.

– But dear God, Gilly, I said, turning to her, it's autumn. Everything starts to die in the autumn.

Sharp glance here from young sprig at her visibly decrepit progenitor.

– Yes, I do speak for myself, I said.

– Oh, don't be so ridiculous.

She turned away. She opened a cupboard. She spoke over her shoulder.

– Percy thinks we might go to Spain.

– *Spain?*

– Honeymoon, Pa – had you forgotten?

She was pouring rice into a saucepan.

– No, I said. Of course. Your honeymoon.

I rubbed my face. I groaned. The tedious abandonment scenario flickered predictably to life for a second or two, and I even glimpsed the moment when Dolores López took her leave of me. Her I saw weeping by the front door in her black overcoat with a suitcase at her feet.

– *Lo siento, Señor Francisco, pero ¿qué puedo hacer? No puedo quedarme más aquí.*

What can I do? she says. I can't stay here any more.

I knew why, of course, bloody ghoul, driving her mad. Driving her out. Then it would just be *me and it—*

Is this how it ends?

But we hadn't got there yet! We hadn't lost Gilly yet, either, although God knows, I thought, it won't be long now. Then she said something that truly astonished me.

– Percy thought you might like to come with us.

150

– What?

– To Spain.

– On your *honeymoon*?

– Yes, Pa. We'd like you to come with us. Will you think about it, please?

I didn't know whether to laugh or cry. I may have done both. On their *honeymoon*? Gilly sat down at the kitchen table and began rapidly to chop a bunch of parsley, *snick snick snick snick.* And I stood with my back to her, gazing through damp eyes into my sodden rotting bedraggled old garden with no Henry in it.

– Percy thinks it might do you good.

– And you, Gilly? I said. What do you think?

– Oh, Pa.

Slowly I sank onto a kitchen chair. I covered my face with my hands and rubbed my eyes. I remember all this very clearly.

– Oh, Pa, what?

I'd made a decision many years before that I would never set foot in that accursed land again. That's not strictly true. That decision was made for me. There was no conscious agency. Simply I knew I could never return.

– Rather late in the day for me, Gilly.

– Percy doesn't think so. Anyway, it's changed.

– What has?

– Spain.

I had to say no. Take your father on your honeymoon? I said. No. Absurd idea. No.

33

HENRY'S BACK! OH, he's come back. He sauntered in through the garden this morning as though nothing had happened. I wept with relief. I went down into the garden to welcome him home. He permitted a few caresses and a bit of silliness from his besotted old friend and provider, and I asked him if he knew what he'd put me through, and he said, in his own inimitable fashion, for he is a cat: Frankly, my dear, I don't give a damn. Somewhat battered, a little bloody round the chops, somebody's biffed him, serve him right for going off like that. There's a big black tabby down the end of the square with a nasty temper, but I like that he's up for a rumble still. Here comes a wave of nostalgia, and it's rather like seasickness.

– Why did your mother leave? said Hugh.

You see! Ten minutes in, and he's moved on to Mummy. Sometimes I'd like to strangle him with his own bloody shoelaces. He's the one who took my poems, of course. I'm sure of it now. I haven't confronted him yet but he'll have to give them back. They're all about Doc Roscoe. He can't just publish them in the *Manchester Guardian*, he doesn't own the copyright, I do. We'll have it out one of these days and I dread it. He'll feel ashamed of himself and he may flounce out and never come back. That would be very terrible. But it might be more terrible never to see those poems in print. Anyway I don't know if I could stand it, him flouncing off, I mean, since he's coming to Gilly's wedding with me. I haven't asked him yet but why would he refuse?

We are drinking tea in the sitting room for a change, everyone else is out. I find it easier to talk if I walk around the room. I pause at the bookshelves, I smell the flowers, I touch the little marble faun Gilly brought back from Boston that time. Hugh is wearing a scarlet tie with two or three tiny diamond motifs in it. How vulnerable I am, it is the bane of age and not the only one.

– But why do you talk to me about Mummy? I say.

He raises his hands, palms spread wide, eyebrows lifted, shoulders also, as though to say, no reason, why not, we must. I gaze at him, I think with a kind of helpless entreaty, it's what I feel – spare me this! Spare me, please. You start me talking about my mother, I may never stop. She was the only source of unconditional love I ever knew! But how is that possible? you say. She ran off with a man when you were still a child. She may not always have been present, I will reply, but a boy knows.

34

For I have always been rather hard to love, you see. It is because I am a divided man. Yes. Half Romantic poet, half man-of-the-people, although now of course I am neither. Half homosexual. Half woman, I used to think. We grew up in a large house in the countryside near Bracknell, and I tell you this now because Hugh has started me thinking about it. Daddy worked in a hospital in Slough. He was head of the Department of Cardiology. I was happy enough as a boy, although I suppose I was aware that Mummy was miserable because I remember how we crept upstairs, Finty and I, one afternoon, to listen to her crying and screaming in her and Daddy's bedroom, and Finty put her finger to my lips so I wouldn't make a sound. Later I asked her why Mummy was screaming and she told me it was because Daddy was mean to her.

It was very bad in the house after that.

When we moved to Cleaver Square Daddy had a new job but it didn't make him happy. This was clear to us all. I think now that we never saw him happy. What a tortured man he must have been. Mummy was very hard on him. She could be terrifying, but never to me. But the older I grew the more I tried to avoid him. Finty told me he didn't see the point of children. She heard him say it to Mummy.

– And what did she say? I said.

– She said, oh, Donald, don't be so ridiculous, said Finty, pretending to be Mummy, which made me hoot.

It was that time in England when the old ways of class authority were crumbling and the implications for me were considerable. If I saw Mummy as a leading lady, I saw my father as a kind of dictator, and there came a day when I was able to challenge him, for when he was drinking it was easy to argue and mock and laugh at him. I remember he demanded an apology for some particularly foul remark I'd made and I refused.

– I'm your *father*! he said through clenched teeth.

– So what? I said.

– It means something, don't you understand that?

– Not to me.

– I should smack you for that.

– Just you try.

It's not pleasant to recall conversations like this. I had no right to such arrogance, and of course there came a day when I found myself bereft of arrogance, and courage. It took me a long time to understand my father but by then it was too late. When he became seriously

155

ill as a result of the years of hard drinking, none of us was heartbroken except Finty. Mummy had run off with Roger Dixon years before but she stayed in touch with us although she didn't come back to Cleaver Square again. I'd always meet her somewhere else. Her glamour never faded, in my eyes. By then I was at Cambridge and writing poetry and going to meetings to discuss what was happening in Russia, then later in Germany and Spain. I had become a socialist, of a sort.

– What sort? said Hugh Supple.

– The shallow sort.

Who then was that shallow, callow fellow, that aspiring poet, that bourgeois man-of-the-people? I do not recognise him now. I have photographs of him, far too many, but he is a stranger to me. Time has alienated us, me from him, as has life, and I find it hard to think we share any kind of identity because I don't know in what, specifically, that identity might inhere. I can't read his poetry, that's certain. Not until I left Spain and grew jaded in the war years, which I spent in London in the ARP – yes, driving an ambulance, all I was good for – did I begin to write anything bleak and dark enough for my later taste. By then the only poetry I read or wrote was heavily inflected with irony, and caustic humour, and nihilism.

I tried to give myself over to pleasure for a time. I allowed the various splits and fissures in my shabby nature to show through. I was suffering a broken heart. That was the core fissure in me, and who was it broke my heart? An American doctor, yes, Doc Roscoe, and how did he break this tender heart of mine? By dying against a wall in front of a firing squad in Spain, when I should have been beside him. Or standing there instead of him! I only ever told Mummy. She didn't take me very seriously. She said, don't worry, darling, there'll be another man. There's always another man. I couldn't even tell her the whole truth, I mean about what happened that night in the monastery, when they took us down the cloister while the bell clanged above us, and then out to the courtyard. How he had looked at me as I turned away, and that what broke my heart was the fleeting reflection I saw then of myself.

35

IT IS THE last day of October. Every year on this day
I visit the grave of my second wife. Gilly's mother,
Noreen. There is a small church, All Souls, not far from
the Imperial War Museum, with a cemetery behind
it which few people know about. Noreen often took
flowers from the garden to lay on the graves of strangers
there. She would have preferred to live in the country,
and asked me once if I would sell the house in Cleaver
Square, but I have always felt a responsibility to maintain
this house despite all the bad memories, I mean to the
extent that it *has* been maintained. When Noreen fell
ill, and it became clear that she would not survive her
illness, she told me she wished to be buried in All Souls.
She was on good terms with the priest and I was able
to secure a plot. I bought a second one while I was at
it and reserved it in my own name. Gilly doesn't know

about this yet. I suppose I'll tell her when the time comes, if it's not too late, ha.

But it was in those years after the war that I began to make a name for myself as a poet, and in particular for a long narrative romance published by Hyperbole titled *The Rapids* which I was told Auden had liked. A few weeks ago I came across it in a cardboard box. One section particularly moved me, and by the time I'd read it through twice I was in tears. I had to go upstairs for a lie-down. The reason is not hard to find. It was all about a near-death by drowning in Spain.

Even now it gives me anguish. Hugh has been sniffing around. He knows there's something there but I won't talk about it. He shall not have him. He is mine.

36

I HAVE NOT been sleeping at all well since I visited Noreen's grave. I wept, of course, which will come as no surprise to you by now, *estimado lector*, but I couldn't seem to shake off the melancholy that descended upon me afterwards. I trudged home through the wind in my winter coat, and although I had planned to drop in at the Rochester and lift a glass in memory of that good, put-upon woman, who had the ill luck or the poor judgement to marry me, but who had at least enjoyed a few good years with Gilly, I found I was in no mood for it, for I suspected Hugh Supple was expecting me, because he knew what I did every 31 October; I had told him. Instead I went to bed, and found that poem of Wystan's, 'Funeral Blues', with its North and South and East and West, and – *I thought that love would last forever: I was wrong*. How perfect a line is that? I never wrote a line that good. I read the poem twice then fell asleep.

Later Gilly asked me if I'd been to Noreen's grave.

– Did you go to Mummy's grave, Pa? she said.

– I did.

– You look awful. Was it very bad?

They were not frequent, but there were moments when Gilly gave me her full warm filial attention. This was one of them. How sweetly concerned about me she was. And she'd had her hair done. It fell fetchingly either side of her pale, beaky face like a schoolgirl cut, with a fringe over her forehead, and the blonde a touch lighter if I wasn't mistaken. And her skin seemed to have cleared up; this not unrelated, I think, to the recent absence of the *generalísimo*. *Ojalá*, long may it continue. No, I told her, it was not so very terrible, but I did feel sad that her life hadn't been happier.

– And you blame yourself for that. But I don't think you should, Pa.

Where did *this* come from? We were in rather deep waters all of a sudden.

– I was not a good husband, Gilly.

– Oh, good husbands, she said. No such thing.

– And good wives?

– We're made differently, that's all.

This was generous, and I hadn't heard my briskly pragmatic daughter speak this way before. It occurred to me that she was in love.

– So are you coming with us to Madrid? she then said.

Oh, Madrid now, is it?! The word *Spain*, that was an abstraction, it was vague. It contained multitudes. But *Madrid*. Things happened to me in Madrid, before all the horror. I knew the sounds of Madrid, the smells, the buildings, the taste of things. I was briefly awash in Madrid and I had to sit down.

– *Madrid*, I murmured, the slurry way the *madrileños* said it, the lispy first *d* and the fiercely clipped second one. I had once heard a flamenco guitar being so sweetly, so movingly played in Madrid, as bombs fell in the distant suburbs, then when the planes got closer the music abruptly ceased, and instead there was shouting. I saw a middle-aged man fall in the Gran Vía and his wife sank to her knees beside him, weeping. He'd been shot dead. To see Madrid again before I died, this seemed suddenly of vital importance to me and I became elated and impatient and I didn't properly understand why.

– Yes, I said, I do want to.

– Really, Pa?

– Now, Gilly, I said, are you sure you mean it? What about Percy?

– It was his idea.

I stood up. To say that it changed everything would be an understatement. Why did it change everything? Because I was haunted and I would never be free unless I went to Madrid. Or because I was wrong to think I had more than enough memories of Spain. Or because I lacked the courage; as once before I had lacked the courage. I didn't say any of this to Gilly. Suddenly restless, I wandered about the kitchen and Gilly sat at the table, watching me. I opened the door of the fridge. There was a bottle of champagne inside. I took it out, then put it back again. I sat down.

– It was Percy's idea?

– He said, man falls off horse.

– Man falls off horse?

– He has to get back on or he'll never ride again.

So I had Percy to thank. As for Gilly, to her it can't have been a welcome idea. Could it? No. But no. No no no. I would have to say no. Take your father on your honeymoon? – absurd idea. No.

37

WE FLEW OUT of London Gatwick on 19 November 1975. The party comprised Hugh Supple, Dolores López, the happy couple and myself. Some honeymoon. *Qué idílico.*

The wedding had not taken place as planned in Westminster Cathedral, that neo-Byzantine monstrosity of striped brick and stone situated where once had stood a fine House of Correction for indolent paupers, also where a man convicted of attempted sodomy was incarcerated in the late 1700s, one Samuel Drybutter. I have been an indolent pauper myself, so I have some sympathetic connection here. I might even have been guilty of attempted sodomy, although it seems unlikely. I usually got away with it.

The priest Gilly wanted to perform the ceremony was her parish priest, Father Jeremy Sandal, a Jesuit, affiliated with the Church of St Francis Xavier on

Horseferry Road. For occluded reasons of ecclesiastical propriety, Father Sandal was not permitted to celebrate Holy Matrimony in the cathedral. So Gilly was married in St Francis Xavier. After the ceremony the guests, I almost said ghosts, some forty of us, crossed the river for a reception in Cleaver Square, Percy's house in Lord North Street being under scaffolding at the time. The weather was unseasonably warm. Many took their drinks out into the garden, where they enjoyed the autumn sunshine, if not the garden itself, after the depredations it had suffered some weeks earlier on account of the ghoul. There was a strong odour of Spanish jasmine in the air and a number of the guests remarked on it. The wife of a former Cabinet minister appeared to suffer a strong allergic reaction, and had to lie down in Gilly's bedroom with watery eyes, sneezing and a runny nose.

I went upstairs and prepared a small shot of adrenaline. But the lady had a terror of needles, and preferred to suffer her symptoms unmedicated.

I had walked Gilly down the aisle. A proud moment, of course, and I was glad Hugh Supple was there to see it. She was in a beige two-piece suit, having decided that the traditional wedding gown was inappropriate for a woman of her age. But she did wear a veil, which she lifted demurely, smiling, when Percy was told he might kiss his bride. Another proud moment for her papá, and I was only sorry that Noreen could not be there. The wedding march was Wagner's and although the organist did her best to mutilate it, the memory of Doc

165

was aroused, for he loved Wagner, and the tears I shed were not entirely for Gilly, nor for Noreen, nor even for Doc. I had decided that a gracious benevolence should be the tone of my performance, and permitted myself no champagne at all and only five or six small glasses of sherry.

I nodded, I smiled, I made amusing small talk. My sister Finty McNulty was on sparkling good form and had found in the wardrobe in the attic a dress she'd last worn in 1929 and saved from moths. She announced that although she was not going to Madrid with the rest of us, she believed that all good marriages began with the attendance of the family in the marital suite. Hearing this, Dolores López made the sign of the cross. She was in stiff black skirts, with a blood-red rose in her oiled, pitch-black hair. She remained close to me throughout the proceedings, I thought at first because she needed my custody. Later I realised it was because I needed hers.

I suspect Gilly was responsible for this arrangement.

I had given the bride away, and Father Sandal, absurd in festive vestments of silver and white, conducted the ceremony with a measure of Jesuitical wit. Ha. There were several senior people from both the Foreign Office and the House of Commons, also friends of Gillian and Percy from Cambridge, the City and elsewhere. I knew most of them. All agreed it went off well. As I say, the weather was dry and bright, a perfect crisp autumn Saturday in London, to the relief of everybody, not least myself.

So yes, I nodded, I smiled, I accepted the congratulations of my guests and confirmed that I was indeed of the party that was to accompany the happy couple to Madrid next week. I had positioned myself close to the fireplace, for the day may have been bright but later in the afternoon it was no longer warm, and from the fireplace I kept an eye on the comings and goings of my guests. I was afraid that there might appear an uninvited guest, and you may imagine who that was.

I didn't see him until late in the proceedings. Dusk was descending and our guests were beginning to leave. I was standing at the French windows with a view of the garden, which possesses a maudlin, almost lachrymose quality in autumnal twilight, very much to the taste of an old Romantic like myself. Like Dolores I had dressed in the manner of times past, a morning suit of blackest serge over a high, white, wing-collared dress shirt. Standing, then, tall, formal, elegant to a degree, a glass of tawny sherry in my pale fingers, and the last of the daylight catching the crystal facets in its stem, I turn towards the garden, and – he is there.

He is there. Or rather: it is there. Indistinct, yes, and to the unsuspecting eye only a smudge, perhaps, just the merest hint of presence, the shadow of a former self, yes, but an avatar of death all the same – the ghoul. Watching the gaiety of a well-lit room from which it would be forever excluded. A small shapeless thing this time, rather than a distinct bodily form, a decaying thing of darkness, and in the dying light of day somehow *viscous*; that is, with a dripping quality to it. Not large, not much larger than a child, in fact, and the features barely distinct in a small, ill-shaped head but the eyes a source of some smeared, vaguely bleary light, within this murky thing of viscous clay, so it seemed, but to Dolores López and myself entirely recognisable although not, surely, to anyone else. Recognisable, and not horrible or frightening because so evidently lacking in definition, animus or force now, even as it seemed almost to smoulder, and give off into the dusk a coil or two of thin black smoke. I was too far away to smell that black smoke but I would wager it was noxious, an *olor furtivo*. I was aware of Dolores López beside me, in her stiff black skirts, and I saw that she saw it too.

– *No es nada*, she murmured.

This I liked.

– *De veras*, I said, turning to her as the coiling smoke disappeared in the thickening darkness. *No es nada*.

And when I turned back to the garden I saw she was right: nothing was there.

But what *had* been there? It occurred to me that perhaps it wasn't the *generalísimo* at all. No. It might have been Noreen, poor Noreen, a rather unconvincing ghost, alas, but risen from her grave in All Souls to come home, and see her only daughter, wed at last.

38

I HAD SOME idea what awaited us in the Spanish capital. The *generalísimo* was in very poor health indeed
and not expected to last much longer. They said he
was a shadow of his former self. So was that what I'd
been seeing in the garden, the shadow? It certainly
explained why he could be in two places at once. I
had half a mind to explain this to Gilly, who as you
know had insisted from the first that he could not
possibly be in Madrid and London at the same time.
I wanted to suggest to her that he could be, if one of
him was the shadow of the self he'd left behind, that
is, his former self. But why burden a woman newly
married with such nonsense? I am not so fatuous as
that, despite whatever other conclusions you may have
reached about my character.

And Gilly – she was happy. She was radiant. It had
not occurred to me how much she wanted this marriage.

I believe she may have given her heart to William Culvert when she was younger, and that he had trifled with it. I think she was treated very shabbily by that man, and I believe she may have resigned herself, in the wake of heartbreak, to a spinster's sad fate. She had returned to Cleaver Square, and had quite possibly assumed she would spend the years of her maturity caring for – me. I know. Absurd. As if I needed it. As if I deserved it, more to the point. So several cheers for Sir Percy Gauss.

As for the honeymoon, and the small crowd that had been assembled so as to escort the happy couple to their bowered bed of bliss in the Hotel Palazzo, on the Calle de Alcalá, I mean myself, and Hugh, and Dolores López, this was apparently what Gilly wanted. She was only sorry, she said, that Finty wasn't of the party, but Finty had put her foot down and said it was absurd to all troop off in a crowd. But Gilly said it was the Spanish way and she was right. The honeymoon was a familial event, in Spain, *la luna de miel*, and there would be time enough for husband and wife to be alone together in the months and years to come.

Hugh Supple was perfectly ready to accompany us to Madrid, having murmured something to do with his article about me perhaps becoming a *book* – God forbid – but I did not take this seriously. And as for Dolores López, to my surprise she hesitated for not a second when the idea was first suggested. Why had we never thought of it before? She had been a child when she left Spain, and now she was a middle-aged woman. In

170

the deep-shrouded silence of her arcane and enigmatic being, had she yearned to see again the land of her birth – could this be so? Nobody knew. But she hesitated for not a second.

39

THE GHOUL NEVER entered the house again, but is still to be observed in the garden these last days before we leave for Madrid. I always know when Dolores López has seen it. She has a way of fixing her eye upon me with an expression that is literally haunted, which I do not think implies reproof – she is not saying that this is all my fault – rather, simply that it is out there, manifesting, as one might speak of some exotic migratory bird, prone to making a loud cheerful display to attract a mate. *It is displaying*, is what she means with that grim black-eyed glance of foreboding as she passes me on the stairs, or turns to me from the kitchen stove, while preparing our frugal meal. It is displaying.

What intrigues me, though, and gives me hope that soon we will be rid of it forever, is the question, what will befall it when the man himself has gone? And it will not be long now. Percy has been very clear about this. The night before our departure he and I sat in my study, drinking whisky and smoking cigars, Gilly having gone out on some last-minute errand.

– The prognosis could not be worse, he tells me; the man is falling apart. There's the Parkinson's, for which he's heavily medicated, but one still sees the hands shaking uncontrollably when he does appear in public. Which is rare, as he's exhausted. He also has phlebitis, and peritonitis, I don't know what else. Stomach ulcers. He's dying, so of course he's exhausted.

We ponder this in comfortable silence.

– Hard work, Percy adds, dying – as though he's done it once or twice himself, and found it an effort.

I accept another of his thin cigars and take immoderate pleasure in it. Not a thing Gilly would permit, were she at home.

– Is he running the country still? I ask.

I know the answer but I want to hear Percy's snort of scorn.

– Is he hell. There's nothing in there, Francis. Vacant. Open-mouthed. Dribbling. People in the Embassy have seen him, they say it's pitiful. He can barely write his own name. He's only appeared once, that was for his granddaughter's wedding to Alfonso de Borbón. Now that man *is* a nasty piece of work.

– Oh?

– The succession may not work out quite as smoothly as we'd hoped, says Percy darkly.

So yes, for Percy, and the Embassy, it is of the utmost importance, the matter of the succession: for upon it

173

depends the future of Spain, a problem not dissimilar, I suggest, to the one my own generation recognised in 1936, the choice then facing Spain being between democracy, the republic, on the one hand, and on the other – the other thing. I need hardly remind you of *that*, I tell Percy.

– No indeed, he says solemnly.

I do love to hear a man of the world speak with authority about matters of policy and statecraft. I could listen to Percy talk about the Spanish succession all night. He tells me that whenever the old man bestirs himself to attend a Cabinet meeting, the sight of Carrero Blanco's empty chair will have him in tears in seconds. It is hard to hear this and not feel a pang. And how very curious, I then think, that one should discover, in age, within oneself, a fount of compassion previously unsuspected – why is this? Because one has turned into a maundering old fool, I suppose.

– Hugh, I said, on our way to the airport the following morning, do you think of me as maundering?

– Oh, no question, he said. Why do you ask?

I did not dignify that with an answer.

40

A s we buckle our seat belts and settle down for the brief flight to Madrid-Barajas, I ask the rather sour stewardess if I might possibly have a large gin and tonic. I am thinking about our conversation last night, Percy's and mine. So the *generalísimo* has a granddaughter, one of several, who has married a 'nasty piece of work', and it worries the British Embassy. How very interesting. You see, I have forgotten my own troubles at the prospect of this Spanish trip. A large part of Percy's worry now is the old man's inability to control the various plots and conspiracies swirling around him in El Pardo, the royal palace, where he dodders about making bad errors of judgement and becoming ever more ill and exhausted. *El cansado*, they call him. The tired one.

I know how he feels. Fortunately I don't have a crumbling Fascist state to hold together, one which is seriously threatened *from within*; nor the urgent problem of naming a successor to my throne. And as the situation deteriorates, according to Percy, the *generalísimo* becomes weaker, ever more isolated, ever more incapable of recognising himself and the members of his Cabinet for the fossils they are, as they blunder through a landscape that is rapidly changing before their befogged and bleary eyes. It is said that he's trapped in the civil war still, as he sanctions more executions, at times involving the *garrote vil*, which has scandalised the entire civilised world and enraged his own people. Meanwhile he is doing less and less work, and his face has taken on a ghastly blankness, as his step becomes increasingly unsteady – and it sounds to me as though he's coming to resemble that shadow of his former self, I mean the ghoul in my garden.

Terror squads carry out their grisly work as new forces of the far right flourish, notably Fuerza Nueva, a neo-Nazi outfit, Percy tells me, while at the same time the universities are becoming more restive, and even members of the *priesthood* have radicalised!

Not a comforting picture then, the one Percy Gauss sketches for me. Violent unrest on all sides as one decrepit old man, clinging to power, tries to chart a course between progressive and hardline factions in his government, while the people of Spain clamour ever louder for change.

Percy thinks it a most interesting moment to visit the capital, and I have to say I rather agree with him! Life in the old dog yet, you see, despite everything – and Gilly too is keenly alert to the import of the moment, as is Hugh Supple, who is a journalist of course. And as for Dolores López, what she thinks is anybody's guess. I tried to tell her it might be dangerous in Madrid.

– *¿Qué más hay de nuevo?* she says.

Roughly translated: What else is new?

We turn south over the Bay of Biscay and soon see below us the Sierra Guadarrama, where I once brought an ambulance through narrow twisting mountain roads, passing only mules and shepherds, a sheer cliff to one side of me and a plunging gorge to the other, while at all times keeping an eye out for German aircraft, which would not hesitate to attack a convoy despite the large red crosses on the roofs of the ambulances below.

I sit at the window of a descending aircraft, the roofs and spires of Madrid visible now. Soon we are entering the city on the Calle de Alcalá, and then to the hotel, and Percy on the pavement is seeing to our suitcases in the cold sunshine and speaking to our driver, Norman, a man from the Embassy, while I stand distracted, thinking of other times, and am overcome, almost, with nostalgia and, too, the confused bitterness I had almost forgotten I still possessed. But I remember the voices on the Gran Vía, and the crowds in the Puerta del Sol, and in the dark, steep Vía Montero, where I lived for some weeks, or *loved*, I almost said.

Then up the steps and into this smart, grand old hotel, nothing but the best for Sir Percy, of course. And it is then I feel the lassitude of the last weeks lifting. I remember what it was to be in this city when its people were besieged, starving, desperate, but displaying every intention of holding out to the end, oh, and the most bitter of ends it was, as the fighting went on in the Casa de Campo and the university buildings by the Manzanares. An old porter in smart uniform stands by the desk, a young man beside him ready to take our suitcases, and I peer at him, curious to know what he was doing here forty years before. We may have shared a bottle, he and I. But he nods to me without recognition, then Gilly turns from the counter and asks me if I want to lie down.

– Lie down? I cry. I'm going out!

She looks doubtful.

– Darling, I know my way around. Hugh?

Percy then joins us and says he supposes I want to get out and have a look around, so why don't we all meet in the bar in an hour and have a bite to eat?

– Pa, don't you even want to unpack?

But I was halfway across the lobby by then, with Hugh Supple beside me. We were glad of our overcoats, our scarves and hats, and with hands plunged deep in pockets we walked briskly, Hugh and I, up the Gran Vía towards the park, El Retiro, which I'd seen earlier from the car coming in and remembered it well. I wanted the blood moving in these creaking joints and limbs, I wanted the sap rising in this wintry old tree I'd become; I wanted, I suppose, to turn the clock back and to be marching with the Brigade through the Puerta del Sol in those heady early days.

I'd left Madrid before the war ended and I didn't see the city fall. There was little yet to suggest the momentous change about to occur here, but I was conscious of a quiet euphoria in the prudent silence of the city, as we walked down empty streets, past shuttered doors, under windows with blinds pulled down, beneath high bare trees on the Paseo del Prado. But it was very cold, I was shivering in my thick coat and I told Hugh I had to go indoors and get warm. We entered a small bar in a side street, where I collapsed.

Yes. Suddenly I felt so very faint and I didn't know why. The cold, I suppose. All I remember is that as I sat down I blacked out. I came to, seconds later, with my head on the table. Hugh was rubbing my shoulders and murmuring my name, saying, Francis, sit up. He seemed relieved to see me open my eyes. The proprietor, a small, tough grizzled old fellow, produced a glass of cognac.

   – *¿Qué pasa?*
   – *Se desmayó.*
   – I fell?
   – *No, señor, usted desmayó en la silla.*

I had fainted in the chair, it seemed, and was unconscious for a few seconds. Most strange. It had never happened to me before. The place was empty. There was a narrow zinc bar under a florid mirror and a few small round tables on the bare planked floor. Nobody else in there but us. It was past the lunch hour. No cognac, I said, I wanted a glass of wine. *Por favor, un vaso de vino tinto*, I said. Hugh sat staring at me, frowning. I set my elbows on the table and sank my head in my hands. When the old man served me the wine he asked me where I was staying and Hugh told him, and he and Hugh went to the telephone and then I saw there was a girl behind the bar gazing at me. I nodded and she smiled. I drank a little wine and felt better. Some minutes later Gilly appeared. Oh God.

– It's nothing, I said.

I tried to get to my feet.

– Stay where you are, Pa, said Gilly.

I appealed to Hugh.

– I was a little faint, that's all. It was the cold.

– Do you need a doctor? said Gilly.

– Christ no! Just give me another minute.

We sat at the table as I drank my wine and Hugh told Gilly what had happened, how I suddenly got so very cold. I could see what she was thinking, that this was a bad idea, the whole thing. I gathered my strength, or tried to. The resilience on which I had so long depended seemed to have deserted me, and at the worst possible moment. Now this nonsense.

– I think we need a taxi, said Gilly, turning to Hugh.

Then she was at the counter and trying to pay, but the old man was refusing to take her money. When we got back Gilly took me up, and I insisted I was fine now, and for God's sake, this was supposed to be her honeymoon. I should never have come but here I was, and Hugh with me, his purpose rather vague, I think, to Gilly, although she behaved perfectly courteously to him. She ordered me to bed. I still felt cold, and rather tired and shivery, and not really very well at all, and a bit sorry for myself, so I went into the bathroom and

changed into my pyjamas and then got into bed. So
much for the hero's return. I'd barely lasted an hour.

Gilly had drawn the curtains and now stood at the
door with her finger on the light switch. I tried to tell her
that her mother had appeared at her wedding reception
but she didn't hear me.

– Go to sleep, Pa, she murmured, and turned the light
off, and the door closed behind her.

41

BYRON WAS OF course the great man in those days, I mean to those of us poets who like himself were prepared to die for a foreign cause. And some did. Ralph Fox, John Cornford, whom I knew. Christopher Caudwell. Julian Bell. To name but four. By December 1936, if I'm right, a British company of about 150 men had joined a battalion of the International Brigades, as meanwhile the Fascists sustained their assault on Madrid but with no real breakthrough. This was after the heavy fighting south-east of the city, which was when I met Doc. The Germans were bombing the city night and day, and Franco's troops were pushing in from the west, but suffering heavy losses, so they decided instead to dig in where they were, and the siege of Madrid properly began then—

All this drifting through my sleeping mind, and I slept through that first day, after collapsing in the bar, and all night, and I didn't wake up until the following morning. As I lay blinking in the daylight that was streaming in from around the heavy curtains, there came a tap on the door and it was Hugh.

– I think you should get up, Francis, he said.
– Yes, yes, what is it, dear boy?
I could hear it in his voice, the urgency.
– It's over.
– No! When?
– Late last night.
Then I was clambering out of bed as best I could, and asking why I hadn't been awakened, why did I not hear bells ringing? We should be out in the streets already—

Hugh was amused. Just get dressed, he told me, and come downstairs. It's on the television.

183

42

I HAVE MENTIONED Goya. I had brought him with me to Madrid, my battered and beloved copy of *Los Caprichos*. These are the engravings inspired by the Terror in Paris, at the end of the French Revolution, which for Goya had occurred only ten years earlier. People have remarked that the great man's self-portrait, in a Bolívar hat – which in my copy of *Los Caprichos* is Plate 1 – bears a resemblance to my own head in profile. My nose is finer than the master's, more of a beak, in fact, *un pico*, but in the sad, wise eyes, and the hint of a justified arrogance, the discrimination evident in the lift of the head and the glance and the set of the mouth, there you have me, I'm afraid. It is a just comparison.

I was eager to visit again the artist's so-called 'Black Paintings', which are housed in a room of their own in the Prado. So I went out alone early one morning, and when I found them they were as I remembered them.

The room was empty of any other visitors. In fact much of the city was empty. Was it caution, in the wake of the death of the *generalísimo*, on the part of the *madrileños*? Or perhaps they were simply supine with relief. I sank onto a bench. I inhaled deeply, for the work seemed to have suffused the place with an unearthly atmosphere I could not at once assimilate.

Avatars of death, these Black Paintings, to my mind: darkness, old age. Guilt. Refugees, lunatics. These painted walls are the walls of death's waiting room. Death was the old señor in the room beyond, who would see you when your turn came. One of the paintings shows two old men, the one shouting into the ear of his deaf companion, saying, What? It's not time yet – but soon! So I imagined it. Others, crowds of helpless grotesques in nocturnal settings of wildness and gloom, with hills and cliffs and distant ruins, in a country where the light is always failing, and there is such madness to be found in the faces, and terror, and idiot glee, that no sense can be made of these crowds of figures lost and insane.

It is the mood of the civil war, I believe, and the years of hunger and violence and terror that followed. Goya saw them coming. He saw it all. Now it was over, and the shock was so great that silence like a fog had fallen on Madrid – how else to understand the mood of the city in those first days after the *generalísimo* died?

A man and a woman, roped together, in a frantic struggle to be free of each other – were they *forced* to marry? And this: 'It seems that man is born and lives

185

to have his substance sucked out of him' – *mucho hay que chupar* – there is plenty to suck.

With this I would concur, oh, with all my heart. I had substance once, see what happened to that!

Bracing stuff. Of course I include here images from *Los Caprichos*, which so nicely complement *las pinturas negras*. I don't know how long I sat there. I was filled with tranquillity, the feeling altogether lacking in any trace of sweetness or mellow *complaisance*, any sentimentality, I mean, for even in their great silence and sadness the abiding impression is of a stark fixed unflinching eye on that reality best known to old people from whom time has scoured the last traces of hope and pleasure, and comfort and illusion: those like Goya who understand solitude, and the absence of compensation. And have been stone deaf since the age of forty-seven. Fear, of course, remains, and guilt, fear not of death but of the experience of dying. For forty years Spain had been dying.

I don't know how long I sat there. I was roused and then routed when a group of schoolchildren were herded in by their teacher, who had them sit on the floor as she began to speak of the greatness of Francisco Goya in the story of Spanish painting. I almost gave voice to my outrage. This was no place for children! – this art was for old men, old women, those who can no longer take nourishment in the normal way. They will choke, these babies, it will sicken them. Get them out of here—! But I said nothing, I slunk off, if the creaky gait of this ancient construct of sticks and joints could ever be called slinking, to find a cup of tea.

186

I visited the Black Paintings once more, and was not disturbed by schoolchildren. Nor did I take Hugh with me, this was no country for young men either. Again, a restless despair not untouched by peace in the presence of last things. I stepped out of the Prado in a state of quiet and calm each time, and the thought, oddly, of being *not alone*. Goya spoke to me down the years, he held my hand as though I were a child myself, and he told me the truth about life and death and guilt and betrayal; but not redemption, not that.

43

OUR SMALL COMMUNITY spent several days in Madrid, and each in his way or her way found the experience agreeable, I believe. Hugh Supple busied himself with visits to museums, and with other research into the history of Madrid in the civil war years. I suspect he intended to place me in historical context when he came to write my biography, and to give precedence to the years I spent in Spain. Occasionally he would ask me a question, as for example about the British machine guns that failed during the Battle of the Jarama. He asked me if I'd like to join him when he visited the Arganda Bridge and Suicide Hill, but I told him I couldn't face it. Too late for me, dear boy, I said.

Percy and Gilly spent hours every day at the British Embassy. I suspect they'd known this would happen, that is, that the *generalísimo* would die and the Ambassador would be required to assist in the work involved in the succession of Prince Juan Carlos. I knew about the committee established to consider British interests when the departure of a dictator was imminent, and a transition to democracy seemed likely. It was chaired by Sir Percy Gauss. In fact the *generalísimo* had seen to the succession. It was the least he could have done. Juan Carlos was the best candidate in the circumstances, although the worst, as soon became apparent, for the old Falange, and the Fuerza Nueva and its terror squads, the Guerrilleros de Cristo Rey. It was suspected by the right that Juan Carlos intended to move Spain in a liberal direction, and it was also suspected that he had concealed his true intentions from the *generalísimo*. For once the right was not wrong. But Percy said there was no guarantee of anything.

– So will Juan Carlos come good? I asked him.

We were in the bar of the Hotel Palazzo, a sombre, warm saloon with panelled walls and deep leather chairs, the kind of room in which Percy feels most at home.

– One can only hope.

There had been much violence in these last years, he said, workers were attacked by ultra-rightist terror squads under the control of Carrero Blanco. May Day of 1973, a policeman was killed during the celebrations, and the right wing was howling for measures of greater repression.

– *Howling*, said Percy, shaking his head a little when he and I discussed these events in the hotel bar, where I was able to smoke one or two of his fine slender cigars unobserved.

– By then we were approaching the crisis, he said.

– And it came?

– Yes. In December. Five days before Christmas.

– The assassination, I said.

– Of Carrero Blanco. You could say that the transition to democracy began then.

We pondered the assassination. We talked of the size of the bomb that lifted the man's car five storeys in the air, and the tunnel beneath the street where the assassins had planted it. It was late but I was not tired. I felt as though a bloody Spanish tragedy, in the opening acts of which I had in some small way participated, had now, forty years on, almost come to an end.

– We are talking of the last days now, I said.

– We are, said Percy Gauss.

I asked him what happened to the *generalísimo* during the last days, what can they have been like? Percy knew everything. He'd been in the Embassy throughout. There had been a heart attack, he said, the third, and some bad pain in his shoulders. And so much of course was wrong already; the phlebitis in his right leg. The gastric ulcers. The blood clots. Problems of both the stomach and the heart. He had caught influenza, and suffered the first two heart attacks. Then came a catastrophic haemorrhage, the carpet and walls of his bedroom literally *drenched* in blood, said Percy. Twenty-four doctors had gathered around the bed of the dying man. They decided to operate.

– Christ alive, I said, to *operate*! But why? On what?

He shrugged. So they operate, he said. It is discovered that an ulcer has opened an artery. The *generalísimo* survives the operation and is put on dialysis, and only then is he moved to a hospital.

On 5 November he undergoes a five-hour operation in which two-thirds of his stomach is removed. He remarks, *Qué difícil es morir*, said Percy. How hard it is to die.

He is put on life support. Days later another massive haemorrhage occurs. His daughter Nenuca has had enough. She believes her father has also had enough, and she orders that he be allowed to die in peace. From the life-support machines the tubes are finally removed.

And early the following morning he dies. It is 5.25 a.m., 20 November 1975. Among the causes cited are endotoxic shock brought on by acute bacterial peritonitis; kidney failure; stomach ulcers; cardiac arrest; bronchopneumonia; thrombophlebitis; and Parkinson's disease. And I might add: severe ethical disintegration.

44

ONE HAD FINALLY to visit El Valle de los Caídos. The Valley of the Fallen. It was where the *generalísimo* would be laid to rest. Ha. Rest: I think not. I told Hugh during lunch, on that strange day when all Madrid was silent with the news of the death so long expected, and so devoutly prayed for, although not by all, by no means all. We were in the dining room of the hotel, which was no less silent than the rest of the city. Not for the first time I desired above all things to know what Dolores López was thinking. I had not long to find out. I gazed at her for a few seconds as with her usual fastidious attention to detail she separated the flesh of the fish she had been served from the bones.

She lifted her head and met my gaze. And then – oh joy! Oh, *ode* to joy! – her black eyes positively flared at me, like a pair of beacons on a dark cliff in a storm at night, a blaze of light in the blackness of each iris which spoke to me as no words could have done of some great movement of the heart, in which I identified *venganza* – revenge! – but more than that, a surge of triumph sweeter even than wine or honey, in which the longed-for downfall of a blood enemy is embraced in celebration in the first full moments of its consummation. It lasted about two seconds.

No sooner had her eyes returned to the fish on her plate than Hugh was leaning into my ear and whispering the words, *Ask about Percy.* Gilly was also preoccupied with her fish, in that silent, high-ceilinged dining room, but she caught the sound of her absent husband's name. Percy himself had been summoned to the Embassy early that morning.

– What are you two plotting? she murmured.

– Do you suppose, darling, I said, that Percy might arrange a car for Hugh and me this afternoon?

– What, today?

– Or tomorrow?

– Oh, Pa. You must realise what it's like there now. She meant in the Embassy, of course.

– Just for a few hours, I said.

– Oh, Daddy, why now?

– That nice man who brought us in from the airport, perhaps? Norman.

– Where is it you have to go in such a hurry?

– El Valle de los Caídos.

If there had been silence in that dining room before, other than the faint clangour of cutlery on white china, with these words, murmured though they were, that

193

silence deepened tenfold. Every fork, tines aquiver, hung poised over its plate, knives likewise. There were nine other guests lunching mutely that memorable day, several Americans among them, and three waiters in attendance upon us. All movement ceased. Twixt plate and lip hung fork and fish. A loaded tray, in passage from kitchen to table, paused on expert fingertips for a second or two. Gilly frowned.

– Why ever would you want to go there now, Pa?

– I will never have another chance.

She was busy with her napkin, touching it to her fishy lips, her eyes elsewhere.

– I can ask him, I suppose.

I leaned across the table and laid my fingers upon hers.

– Thank you, Gilly, I whispered.

– Will it even be open? she said.

– Even if it's not, I said.

45

WE GOT OUR car. Dear Percy. Unflappable Percy. In the midst of crisis, and the body of the dictator not yet cold, could he make time to organise a car and driver for Gilly's father and his faithful factotum? He could. A large car, a black Rover, and with a pleasant friendly driver, the man who'd brought us in from the airport some days before, Norman. Car and driver arrived at the hotel promptly at ten the following morning, and we drove out through empty streets to visit the great crypt in which the body would be entombed some days later.

The day was clear and cold. Hugh was sombre. He was wearing his thick grey overcoat and had a camera on a strap round his neck. He also wore his old school scarf. I too adopted a sombre mien and asked Norman if he would mind turning off the radio. It was broadcasting only funereal death music. Spain was mourning its lost monster.

I had my own mourning to do, and we made a stop in Fuencarral, an ancient town, where in the *cementerio* had been buried those of the British Battalion who'd fallen at the Jarama. I had no great hopes of finding Doc Roscoe's grave. Often enough in the Bull at Smithfield, with men who'd been with me there, I'd heard that after the war Franco had the dead of the Jarama dug up and dumped in unmarked graves, location unknown. Julian Bell was one of them, although he died at Brunete. I knew him. Like me he lost his ambulance and became a stretcher-bearer, but unlike me he got a new ambulance. As he was doing repairs to it there came a Luftwaffe bombardment, and he was hit. He suffered a massive lung wound that opened his chest so deep his beating heart was visible to those attending him. He was the nephew of Virginia Woolf, who had persuaded him not to join the infantry, nor carry a gun, but to be a medic. A *sanitorio*. So much safer, they all thought. Later that night he died.

But the cemetery. On this bleak grey morning we bumped up a rocky hill and found walls of piled stones still standing, but nothing remained of the graves of the men who'd been buried there. A plaque had been raised in their honour, so I'd been told, but it too had gone. Hugh realised that something was badly amiss as I wandered through a desecrated patch of waste ground in the cold light of the day, in the shadow of the mountains, in a sudden eruption not merely of sorrow but a gust of hatred for the man who bore responsibility for all this.

After we had resumed our journey Norman turned his head to address his passengers in the back seat. He quietly told us we would soon have our first glimpse of the greatest crucifix in Europe. I had calmed down somewhat.

– Greatest? I said.

But Norman's eyes were on the road again, and he didn't respond. The sheer height of the thing, when it came into view, filled me with fresh foreboding, and loathing, also a kind of awe, if such a combination of emotions is possible. Five hundred feet tall, I later learned, this crucifix towers over a wild bleak rock-strewn stretch of the Sierra, and as the road climbed we saw that it was rooted in a great heap of granite boulders piled together, over millennia, no doubt, and riven with fissures sprouting dense clumps of pine. Upon these chaotically heaped rocks a platform had been erected around which clustered a gigantic statuary of clinging saints, and it was from this platform that the crucifix soared into the pale wintry sky. In all its bruto-Fascist severity, it was impossible not to be reminded of the architectural manners of the Third Reich.

I murmured this aloud and Hugh at once agreed. I think he was a little worried about me. Mystified by my mood, I think, so broody, so *seething*, had I become, confronted with that broken, empty graveyard, rumours of which I'd heard in the Bull; and how it had angered us all.

197

But everything is huge here, in the Valley of the Fallen, and I understand it is the way of the Fascist architect. The individual is as nothing to the Fascist architect, who likes humanity only in *the mass*. He it is who tears open the tombs of his enemies, and dumps their remains like so much waste. But it is the crypt that draws us now, when at last we are out of the car, and crossing a vast esplanade in a cold wind, on foot; and then led through great doors by way of a basilica into a huge, barrel-vaulted crypt blasted into the mountain at the base of the towering cross, and oh, the idiotic majesty of it all! And does it surprise you to learn that all this, all of it, was the brainchild of the *generalísimo*? No. And at the very heart of it, under the high altar, at the far end of this vast crypt, lies the tomb in which will rest, in glory, unto eternity, in just a few days, his own mortal remains. It's all for him.

It is my contention that I never lost control. And that I acted at all times as a man in full possession of his faculties. They would have none of it, Gilly and Percy I mean. But did they honestly believe I suffered some kind of a seizure?

– I did not suffer a seizure. I have never suffered a seizure, I told Gilly later.

– Pa, what about your nightmares?

– They occur at night. When I am asleep.

– And when you fainted in the bar?

– I was cold and dehydrated.

198

Because, you see, it was in their interest to have it known that old Francis had got himself unhinged by a seizure. It would make Percy's life easier, because he, poor man, was the one who had to extricate me from the mess I was about to make.

46

I THINK IT began with the first glimpse I had of that frightful crypt. I had walked up from the car with Hugh amid a few tourists as far as the esplanade, where I paused, and stared at the really rather disturbing *pietà* atop the great bronze doors that led into the thing. In black stone the dead Christ is attended by a cowled figure whose face is lost in shadow, a most Gothic scenario, with the great cross rising beyond it against the sky, which on this afternoon in late November was growing more heavily clouded in shifting layers of black and grey. It was a wild place devoid of all redeeming spiritual grace or peace, or transcendence, perhaps because it was built by men who hated the *generalísimo*. Republican prisoners of war, I mean, whose long prison sentences could be worked off in days of labour at the rate of three for two. On this day the weather had started clear but then turned windy and cold, and I was touched with dread at the prospect of entering the crypt.

Moving alongside a group of American tourists from a bus, Hugh and I climbed the fifteen wide windswept steps from the esplanade to the round-arched doors of the crypt, vast bronze doors which, according to the guide attached to the tourist group, displayed the fifteen mysteries of the rosary, whatever they might be. The only mystery confronting me was where I might find a drink in this godforsaken place.

Apparently not in the crypt. The guide, a callow Spanish youth, though not without a certain gauche charm, whom we could not help but overhear, was talking about the technical difficulties involved in building a crypt inside a mountain. It seems you run into problems of pressure and stability when you attempt to punch into raw rock what is, in effect, a vast tunnel. But raw rock was the effect the architect apparently wanted, referred to by our young man as the *rupestrian effect*, new word for me. I thought it might help furnish a limerick, and lo, despite my filthy mood, a limerick began to materialise. The builders in the end used concrete for various of the arches that supported the structure, which they then faced with freestone, which we were told was a fine-grained limestone, easy to cut. The finished crypt is almost eight hundred feet long and more than a hundred and twenty feet high. Vast, then – standard Fascist excess – and saints wherever you looked, also archangels, disciples, Our Lady of the Pillar, beatified Dominican monks, and between the concrete arches, which stabilise this barrel-vaulted subterranean chamber of horrors, a series called *The Apocalypse Tapestries*, which I admit did intrigue me a little.

Soon after occurred the disgraceful incident.

The American tourists had been gathered together by the comely youth at the high altar. He was directing their attention to the design of the mosaic tesserae in the dome overhead, which it seems comprised more than five million of the little coloured tablets. It features Jesus Christ himself surrounded by a good many Spanish saints and martyrs, but it gave me a nasty crick in the neck to get even a glimpse of these celestial personages above us, and I turned my attention to the crucified Christ nailed to a rough-hewn cross that towered over the high altar. But enough of these lofty crosses, I thought, for this one too gave me a crick in the neck.

On the floor to the left of the altar was the tomb of José Antonio Primo de Rivera. Him at least I knew about. He founded the Spanish Fascist Party, the Falange. He would keep the *generalísimo* company forever, happy couple, ha.

On the other side of the altar was a long white rectangular marble slab next to a deep hole of the exact same dimensions. It was the expectant tomb of the *generalísimo*, who for what seemed an eternity had been haunting me in my garden, my home and my bed. I stood before it with bowed head. I began to murmur my newest composition.

The effect of raw rock is rupestrian,
Which fact might disturb an equestrian,
Who pissing while riding,
And with rockface colliding,
Limps home in disgrace, a pedestrian.

47

I T COULD HAVE been worse. The tomb after all was empty, although it has to be said – not for long! And the Spanish do have some residual reverence for old men, particularly mad ones. Even so, after the fact, when the guards descended upon me they were not gentle, and despite Hugh's noble efforts to protect me, and the noisy protestations of the Americans, I was quickly hustled off the high altar and down the east transept to a cell in a cloister with a concrete bench in it, onto which I was unceremoniously flung. No real harm done, and I was delighted to hear both Hugh Supple and the young man who'd been leading the tour group, in the cloister beyond, remonstrating about the rough treatment I had received, considering it was an accident, ha. *Es un inglés respetable*, the young man was telling them, *no sabe lo que hizo, no tiene la culpa, ¡es inglés!*

Truth be told, it wasn't the first time I'd been flung into a Spanish cell. Long story short, it took Percy Gauss half a day to rescue me from the irate officers of the Guardia Civil, who had it in mind that I should be prosecuted and possibly subjected to some inquisitorial torture reserved for acts of such heinous sacrilegiosity as the one I committed upon Franco's tomb. But a phone call from Someone High Up took the wind out of their sails, and reluctantly they released me into the custody of the British Embassy, in the person of Sir Percy Gauss.

Percy came in another Embassy car, with a second driver. Gilly was not with him. You may imagine the atmosphere as we drove back to Madrid. He sat up front with the driver. I had the back seat to myself. Hugh returned with Norman. Percy, who was being unchar-acteristically silent, stared at the road ahead, not once giving any sign of his feelings even when he turned, frowning, gazed at me for a few seconds, and turned back. Later he regained his sense of humour.

– At least the bloody thing was empty, he said.

But Gilly was pale with rage. What angered her was my lack of consideration for Percy. Had I no idea how delicate the whole question of the succession was, and how complicated the diplomatic effort being undertaken by the Ambassador and his staff, among whom Percy had taken a senior role despite the fact that he was supposed to be on his honeymoon? What was I *thinking*?

I knew, though, that it was less serious than she sug-gested. The question of the transfer of power from the *generalísimo* to Prince Juan Carlos would not be decided by some mad old boy like me, and the triumph of the gesture was mine alone. My only regret? That the *generalísimo* would never hear about it, or not in this world. It was decided that Gilly and Percy would stay on in Madrid until all the diplomatic issues were settled, while I would be returning to London the following day, with Hugh Supple, in the charge of a young man from the Embassy who was in any case required there for purposes of liaison with the Foreign Office. Dolores had left some days before.

I did it for Doc.

48

I T WAS ANOTHER bitter cold day but the sky was clear, and I awoke a happy man. The car was due at the hotel at half past ten. I was eager to see the Spanish newspapers. I have little time for the press these days, as you know, with the exception of course of the *Manchester Guardian*. Gilly had warned me to speak to nobody – I mean *nobody*, Pa, do you hear me? – but it was hardly the sort of thing one could keep to oneself. It seems the Spanish press had been muzzled, which disappointed me. Many a Spaniard would lift the fist, and grin a happy grin, hearing this news. And him a man of the Republican cause, they would say, who'd marched in Barcelona when the Internationals went home, and was applauded by La Pasionaria herself.

The flight to London was uneventful, as was the train into the city from Gatwick. Hugh was silent. Very cold weather indeed, and a wind that cut like a knife, so I bade farewell to my *compadre* and took a cab home from Victoria. I cannot deny that I had awoken with a slight taste of bathos on my tongue, and it became stronger as the day wore on. I think Hugh Supple did not like what had happened, nor the glimpse we'd been afforded of the Spanish security forces at work. All too easy to imagine other circumstances, and a different outcome.

In fact I was in some pain, for when the guards had seized me on the altar of the crypt and hustled me away they had not been gentle, and there were bruises on my upper arms, vivid purple, like a jacaranda in bloom. I had also taken a brisk hard smack to the back of the head which continued to throb painfully, despite the several aspirin I had swallowed.

There was, too, the humiliation of being expelled from the country in disgrace, which I could certainly have tolerated had it been only the Fascist authorities I had offended. But the British were just as furious, Gilly in particular. What a lot of atonement I would have to perform. And to Hugh as well, for I supposed this would do his journalistic career no good at all, and he might well be rethinking his plans about the book. As for me, it would turn out as I had always feared it would, that is, with abandonment and isolation, also disgrace. Mad, bad, haunted and alone – this was what I had to look forward to now. And I'd brought it on my own head. Nobody to blame but myself. Still, the old boys in the Bull would enjoy the story.

I sank into a state of morbid introspection. Finty in our absence had returned to the Isle of Mull, with no indication as to when or even if she planned to return to Cleaver Square. Henry was nowhere to be seen, probably off sulking somewhere because he'd been left behind. I went up to the attic a few days after I got back, and such a powerful sense of desolation was there, in that long dusty room with its slanting beams and cobwebbed dormers, in the absence of the few personal objects that had created, at least in Finty's mind, an illusion of home. All that remained was the crucifix over the bed, the sight of which at once aroused the memory of the great crossed tree on the high altar of the *generalísimo*'s crypt.

I sat on the bed, where there was only an ancient leaky mattress on the bedsprings now, and my shoulders slumped, yes they did. And did I weep? Of course I bloody wept. A few precious drops fell to the dusty planks and I clutched my face with one hand, and the edge of the mattress with the other, and for some seconds gave myself over to sobs.

Then I heard footsteps. Ascending the stairs, coming up through the house. I sat in a state of some suspense as whatever it was ascended towards the attic, heavier now, *clump clump clump*. I was suddenly very cold indeed. The footsteps ceased. Slowly, the door swung open on its rusty hinges.

– *¿Señor Francisco?*

With bleary eyes I lifted my head. Dolores López!

– Ah, Dolores, Dolores, you are back—

She sat down heavily beside me on the bed, and took my hand.

— *¿Qué hay? ¿Qué le pasa?*

— *Las cosas salieron mal, querida Dolores.*

She wanted to know what the matter was and I said that everything went wrong.

— *¿Cómo?*

— How? I said. I'll tell you.

And I told her in Spanish what I'd done.

— *¿Echaste una meada en su tumba Señor Francisco?* You piss in his grave?

I nodded my head. I pissed in his grave.

Then I felt the mattress heaving beneath me; it had started shaking on its bouncing springs. She was laughing! Dolores López was laughing! Such a thing had never been known before. Silently at first, with her plump hand on her mouth, she shook with mirth and her large sad black eyes were turned on me, shining like a pair of headlights, full beam, until she could hold back her joy not a second longer, and sat back and gave full, free tongue as had never before been heard in this old house, or not to my knowledge — she bellowed, and I am sure her laughter rang through the house and into the basement and quite possibly the length of the garden and I dare say across the square and into the saloon bar of the Earl of Rochester, and beyond—

I gazed at her, and within a very few moments became infected myself, and the mood I had known in the immediate aftermath of the disgraceful incident returned, and the pair of us were soon shouting and hooting as we rocked there on those old bedsprings, and it seemed we would never stop. But at last, damp-faced, and

210

astonished, we allowed the laughter to die. We looked at one another – and up it started again.

It died and revived once more, and then Dolores López rose to her feet, regarded me warmly, spoke my name – *Ah, Señor Francisco* – and left the attic. I sat, exhausted, but feeling cleansed of the shame that had so depressed me since my return from Madrid, and liberated, exalted, even, I listened to Dolores López descending the attic stairs.

After some moments I wiped the tears from my eyes and glanced out of the attic window. Already dusk was descending, and with it a few flakes of snow.

Winter.

49

WINTER.

My last?

How very strange it is without Gilly in the house. I miss her but I am not altogether without company. Dolores López is above stairs more frequently now, and her silent presence is a source of comfort to me. She understands my needs: when I require a pot of tea, when a glass of sherry. She too is dedicated to the welfare of Henry Threshold. And she is of course in an important way *complicit* with me. My accomplice: she saw the ghoul in the garden, if that's what it was. It has suited me to think so, to have constructed some kind of *origin myth* involving a Spanish officer in North Africa who encounters such a creature – or spirit, or entity – and strikes a bargain with it, like Faust. The *generalísimo* traded his soul for a godlike power over life and death, specifically that of the Spanish people. But why, then, in the last months of his wretched life, the ghoul he became should turn up in the garden of an old man in south London who hated him with all the passion of his own ageing, failing spirit – myself, I mean – this remains a mystery, or more probably, as I have come to think, a quirk of fate.

Yes. A quirk of fate. *Quirk*: a word of unknown origin but we understand it well enough. So by some *quirk of fate* this monstrous *generalísimo*, who held to a doctrine that ran counter, violently so, to most accepted ethical doctrines of human life on this earth, and was in this regard no different from any of the other psychopathic demagogues who have tried and will continue to try to annihilate all who do not agree with them – comes to rest in my own modest garden. And here it is that I see him, a blackened, viscous, diminished, formless excrescence, as witnessed by myself and Dolores López during Gilly's wedding reception before we all went to Madrid, where I took the opportunity of pissing in his grave.

Yes. I'm afraid so. The whole lot. All I had, and how it steamed and stank, although he wasn't there to receive it unfortunately. Quite a bit of spatter when they dragged me off, as I tried to do up my fly buttons, and no wonder he wants an apology. But he'd befouled *my* bed, I was quite within my rights.

I did it for Doc, whom I'd so grievously betrayed, and about whom my guilt is a mordant canker which has gnawed at my innards for more years than I can remember, and this I only confess to you now, having deceived you as to my true condition, and pretended a soundness of mind and spirit which I frankly do not possess.

50

A<small>ND THEN, AT</small> the last – a miracle. Yes. It happened three nights later, after an uneventful day marked only by a predictable display of indifference from Henry Threshold, who since my return from Madrid has in no uncertain terms expressed his displeasure at having been abandoned without explanation. I'd asked Johnny from the Rochester to come over and feed him, and it seems Henry has taken a fancy to Johnny, which explains his coldness to me.

Be that as it may. I had fallen asleep soon after eleven, after reading a few pages of Flaubert, the story about the old woman and the parrot. I may have turned off the light or I may not, I don't remember. What I do remember is awakening to a room otherwise in total darkness but for a subdued light around the wing chair, which I have mentioned to you before. It is an old chair which belonged to my father, still sturdy, the upholstery embroidered in gold thread and with curved legs of polished mahogany. It was occupied, and for some seconds I could not make out who sat there, for although I saw clearly enough the crossed legs in loose khaki trousers, the scuffed leather boots, the large strong hands folded in the lap – the upper body and face of my visitor were lost in shadow until he leaned forward. Also there was an unfamiliar and most unwelcome smell in the room: tobacco! Nobody was allowed to smoke upstairs, not even Finty. But I smelled a cigarette and I now saw it hanging glowing from the lip of my silent visitor. For some reason I thought he was an aviator, possibly Ramón Franco, brother of the *generalísimo*, who had come as some kind of an emissary. But that was most unlikely.

I struggled up in the bed as the figure crushed out the cigarette in a plate on the small table beside the chair, and I saw who he was. I was sitting up in the bed now, pushing my fingers through my hair, my eyes wide, and oh, awe, wonder, incredulity, all that, flooding through my startled unbelieving brain. I don't know what I said, I could have said anything. He was rising to his feet now, and where the light was coming from I still couldn't say, and although there wasn't much of it there was enough that what I saw, lit from below, was one side of a destroyed head, with the flesh stripped away and the clean white bone exposed around the mouth and jaw, a few teeth still intact, and the temple, and some part of the skull above the ear.

I sat in my bed gazing at this ruined head of his. I wanted only to apologise!

– Doc, I said – for yes, it was he – there hasn't been an hour of my life I haven't felt so very deeply ashamed of what I did that night—

I also said that if I could have my life to live again I would not turn away, I would take his place against that wall, and die that night as it was intended that I die—

– No need, he said.

His voice! It was then, after he had risen from the wing chair, that he came over to the bed, and laid his hand on my head for a few seconds, then moved towards the door, and the light in the room started to fail, and the outline of his poor shattered head, his upper body, his arms and hands and legs, all were fading.

– No, stop, I cried, struggling to get out of my high bed but it wasn't easy, it was never easy. Wait, will you come back?

From within the gloom into which he had almost entirely disappeared he spoke again.

– No need, he said.

A second later I heard him descending the stairs, and having now got out of bed, and into my dressing gown and slippers, I followed him, and I reached the hall downstairs as the front door opened and a shadow passed through it—

Then radiance – it was dawn. And as a wintry sun rose over the houses, and Doc disappeared into the light, I stood there in the open door, before me Cleaver Square all white with fresh snow shining in the early sun as if it were a great lamp. I became aware that Dolores López had joined me, and then the most extraordinary

216

thing! – we saw through this blinding snowy light a figure arise, face lifted to heaven and arms spread wide, and it was Doc, whole, entire, head and body bathed in the light of dawn, radiant in khaki and canvas, rising out of Cleaver Square and into the light beyond, and faded quite away—

Then when he'd disappeared from view the clouds drifted in, and a few seconds later Cleaver Square was itself once more.

51

A DREAM, YOU think. An apparition, the product merely of a failing mind, an old man attempting in the disturbed depths of his florid psyche to right the wrong that had haunted him for forty years. Explain this then: on the plate on the table beside the wing chair in which the man had been sitting, on that plate I found the crushed remnant of an unfiltered, half-smoked cigarette. Ducados. The brand we smoked in Spain. Rough, cheap tobacco rolled in thin yellow cigarette paper, nothing like it. I brought that half-smoked cigarette to my nose and inhaled the odour. In the drawer of my bedside table is a small silver case in which I once kept a pair of cuff-links, long since lost. Into that silver case I deposited Doc's cigarette.

And would I open that drawer from time to time, and from it retrieve the silver case, and open it to smell that half-smoked cigarette so as to reassure myself as to what had occurred that night?

No need.

52

ENOUGH. I AM almost done. On a clear day I can hear Big Ben strike the hours, have I mentioned this already? And never send to know for whom that bell tolls, old Francis, for you don't want to know. But when Big Ben tolls noon, it tells me it is time I got myself into my scarf and gloves and overcoat to make the epic trek from my own front door to the cheery warmth of the saloon bar of the Earl of Rochester. There I am expected by young Hugh Supple, with whom I will drink one or two small glasses of dry sherry or, if it is an occasion, one of Johnny's stiff ones, a large gin and tonic, the American way. It is the highlight of my day.

And today is no different. The dear boy. I count on the fingers of one hand now the intimates of this, my last winter, and the number is three: Hugh, Dolores López and Henry Threshold. Gilly and Percy are not so far away, just across the river, but I do not see them every day. There are still a few of the old soldiers from the Jarama who convene at the Bull in Smithfield Market, and I join them when I can, and am for once the hero of the hour, the Great Pissant Madge, as Eddie Wargrave calls me. And Finty, dear Finty, will she ever make the long journey south again, as she did last summer, arriving as you remember at dead of night in heavy rain dressed all in black, such that I was convinced she was the incarnation of Death Itself? She writes to me, in fact we correspond with some regularity, and her reflections on her Hebridean existence are not unamusing.

I imagine she will outlive me. Don't trouble to get on a train, dear Finty, to attend the obsequies over my modest coffin – Gilly will probably have that awful Jesuit to officiate in the gloom of St Francis Xavier, so I will not miss you. We will meet again, I don't know where, but perhaps in that Other Place, if such there be, which I very much doubt, unless—

Will you come back? This I had asked him.

No need, he said.

The last days. It's not so bad. And I've been poking around in the garden with a critical eye, and if it's given to me to spend another springtime in this house I believe I could bring it back. The blight I spoke of during the autumn, when I became convinced that the ghoul was sickening not only my garden, but my bed, my daughter – my *life!* – I may have been exaggerating. We need not dwell on it. But yes. It's entirely possible that I exaggerated the whole thing. I am famous for it, exaggerating. I can hear Gilly now.

– Oh Pa, don't *exaggerate* so, for God's sake. It's really not what you think.

What might she be speaking of? Oh anything. It hardly matters now. She's forgiven me for desecrating Franco's grave. I won't say she has come round to seeing the funny side of it – that would certainly be an exaggeration. She was very cross indeed that I put Percy to a bit of trouble, but he, dear man, handled everything with such grace and aplomb that I don't unduly castigate myself for putting him to the trouble. He certainly sees the funny side of it now, and tells me the incident is still spoken of with amusement in the corridors of power. I lose no sleep over it. In fact I sleep rather well these days, and have not been troubled by—

Bong! Bong!

There it is! The first faint chimes coming up the river from hard by the Houses of Parliament, where even now Sir Percy Gauss strives to further British interests in a dirty, bloated world, and all good luck to him.

Bong! Bong!

I really must get my coat on, I hate being late. I think I might have a gin today, that would be just the thing, cold winter morning like this. One of Johnny's stiff ones. And I will toast the memory of Doc Roscoe, with whose ghost I am finally at peace, absolved. I think. If he will have me, that radiant man. That *risen* man.

I might even light a candle in that hideous cathedral on Victoria Street.

Editor's Note

This is the final entry in what I believe to be the last of the diaries of my friend, the poet Francis McNulty. He died in his sleep later that afternoon. Henry Threshold was with him. I say 'diaries': Francis scribbled erratically in a number of lined exercise books, which I discovered in his desk, held together by a rubber band, along with a large buff envelope containing a batch of his late unpublished poetry. Francis's handwriting was erratic at best, at worst illegible. In moods of apparent enthusiasm he failed to stay within the lines.

The writings were not organised chronologically. There are no dates. I have attempted to arrange them in some kind of order, and numbered them as though they were chapters. I am only sorry he is not here to edit them himself.

Francis McNulty is buried in the graveyard of All Souls, a Roman Catholic church in the Borough of Lambeth. He lies beside his second wife, Noreen, mother of his only child, Lady Gillian Gauss. May God rest his eternal soul!

H.S.

Acknowledgements

I'd like to give my warmest thanks to my Spanish teacher, Brooke May, and to my brother-in-law, Jonathan Aitken. And my love as always to Maria, without whom nothing at all would be possible.